Also by Cody Grey Adams

Midlife Crazy
an erotic romance

The Woman Of My Dreams

A ROMANCE

BY

CODY GREY ADAMS

This is a work of fiction. All characters and all specific details of the setting are figments of the author's imagination. This means that any resemblance to actual human beings, institutions, and incidental historic events is coincidental. Historical places and major historic events are mostly left where they occurred or once were.

The limericks included on pages 100-101 are traditional pub fare and reside in the common domain.
The lines of poetry included on page 119 are the opening lines of *The Hound of Heaven* by Francis Thompson and reside in the common domain.

The paraphrased poem about stepping off into darkness on page 121 has been attributed to other writers but was first written by Patrick Overton and published in 1975 in a collection of poems titled *The Leaning Tree*.

ISBN 978-1-933482-69-9

White Turtle Books
Canby, Minnesota
whiteturtlebooks.com

The mass of men lead lives of quiet desperation. What is called resignation is confirmed desperation. From the desperate city you go into the desperate country, and have to console yourself with the bravery of minks and muskrats. A stereotyped but unconscious despair is concealed even under what are called the games and amusements of mankind. There is no play in them, for this comes after work.

Henry David Thoreau, *Walden*, 1854

1

She of a Thousand Faces

She was the woman of my dreams. I knew this the moment I saw her. Nor was there any doubt. Though I had seen her a thousand times as I dreamt of many things, it had never been here and now, in the flesh. She had worn a thousand faces but still I knew she was the one I had been seeking in all the others.

We met at a conference for writers. I was a keynote speaker there and it was just after I had spoken on a Saturday afternoon that I encountered her in person for the first time. She was with a group of other young women but when first our eyes met, we both knew. I saw her eyes widen in surprise and something shifted in the universe. I knew nothing would ever be the same for her, or for me, either.

The fly in the ointment was the fifty years that lay between her birth and mine. Yet that sad fact had little to do with how I felt. The moment it happened the years fell away and in my heart I was a young bull again, pawing the ground and bellowing his challenge. The young men lurking around the cluster of young women heard it in the silence and moved away. As did the other young women with her. The two of us were left alone, she and I, face to face with neither of us knowing what to do about it.

Then I saw fear rise in her eyes as we stood mute, two naked souls who could not hide from the other. Not knowing what else to do, I spoke the simple truth. "You are the woman of my dreams," I whispered. "You have nothing to fear from me."

"I know," she murmured. "That's what scares me. It was me you were talking about wasn't it? I thought so right away but then I thought I was being silly. I thought every woman in the room probably felt that way."

"You have no idea how scary it was for me to say what I did. I have never revealed myself to an audience like that before. It was hard to believe I was saying what I did, and I wondered why I was. Now I know."

"Yes, now you know," she said sadly. "And tomorrow morning we all go home."

"No place will ever be home without you..." I said and then the world intruded. Some star-eyed gusher passing by tugged at my sleeve and I turned to ask them to wait. When I turned back she was gone and my heart lay in ashes at my feet. Within twelve dozen heartbeats I had found she for whom my soul has yearned for most of a century, and had then lost her. I stood there too sad for tears, trembling and alone.

It was then the heavens interceded and I felt the soft touch of an angel on my arm. It was one of the other young women standing with she who had ravished my soul. She had come back for something she left she told me. "Are you all right, Mr. Adams?" she asked, clearly concerned.

"No," I answered sadly. "How could I be? I just found the one for whom I have been looking for all my life and now she is gone."

"You mean the woman of a thousand names? The one you were talking about when you spoke?" She seemed surprised.

"Yes," I told her. "I just met her face to face for the first time ever and I don't even know her name."

The young woman's face cleared and she smiled. "Of course, you do. You were just talking to her a moment ago, weren't you? Her name is Grace."

"Of course it is," I replied, feeling the shards of my heart rise from the dust and begin to coalesce around something like hope. "Grace. What else could it possibly be? Do you happen to know her last name?"

Her laughter was like a silver bell, lifting my spirits like the rising sun on a clear morning after a week of blizzard. "She didn't tell you? It's Adams, the same as yours!"

I could swear I heard the hint of a celestial titter laughing along with her at this doddering wreck I'd become. "Well, there's no fool like an old fool, is there, Rose?" I asked, spotting her name on the tag we all wore to show we belonged. Hers was edged in red and told me she was a facilitator, whatever that might be. Mine was purple, I suppose marking me as royalty for the conference.

"You're no fool, Mr. Adams," she assured me. "I think Grace is a very lucky woman." She looked down, embarrassed. I knew she had heard everything I said to Grace and I felt even more the fool.

"How can you possibly consider her lucky, Rose? I'm old enough to be her grandfather, for goodness sake."

"What does that have to do with anything?" she declared. "If Grace wasn't such a good friend, I'd take a run at you myself!"

"Good God, woman, you're as daft as I am," I declared and she laughed again. "And I'd be fool enough to take you up on it!" I added, not believing what I heard myself saying. Yet it was the utter truth and there was no getting around it.

"Mr. Adams!" she declared, feigning indignation and failing miserably.

"I think you've earned the right to call me Cody, Rose," I replied. Fickle soul that I am I was wondering if she really meant it. It had been a long while since my life had known the grace of a good woman. There had been a number of encounters since Angie died. Some were long, others were not. Only one, the longest, had been close to serious. This had been with a sweet lady from Anthropology, but she got an excellent job offer from Penn State in Altoona.

That had been a couple of years back and there had not been anyone since. The fact is, I was lonely. So I challenged Rose, silly dolt that I am. I had no idea the lady was as crazy as I.

"I mean, propositioning a doddering old fool in a public hallway?" I asked.

Rose gave me a look as old as men and women. It told me she wasn't fooled for a minute. She recognized the resolve concealed beneath my humor and took the challenge. "So what if I am? Would you dare to be taking it, Mister Adams?"

"Are you daring me, then?" I riposted.

"Am I not?" she countered, looking around the hallway before moving close to me, so close I could feel the heat of her breast and loins. I found myself responding as men have from the beginning of time. My answer was a kiss that left no doubt.

"We better find us a room," Rose murmured, looking around the hallway again. Fortunately, it was still empty. Then she looked into my eyes and I knew full well that I was lost.

We ended up going to my room at the motor inn. Then we ended up missing the final banquet that evening. At some point someone called to see if I was all right and I told them I had a touch of something going around. I said that it might be catching and I better stay in bed.

"You're a good liar," Rose observed, eyeing me like a *hausfrau* eying a fresh roast.

"Yes, but an honest one. I make sure those I care about

know when I am lying."

"So am I someone you care about?" she asked shyly. There was a terrible vulnerability behind the question.

"How could I not, Rose?" I asked, taking her in my arms and kissing her tenderly. "You've been terribly generous to an old fool."

I was rewarded with a bawdy wink. "You could have fooled me, ancient one. I've seen a good many young studs who could learn a lot from the master."

"I can see it all now," I told her, outlining a theater marquis with my hands. "The Cody Adams Academy for Inept Studmuffins. Seriously though, grand daughter, you must admit that you gave me plenty of inspiration."

"You mean it wasn't the little blue pills?"

"The ones I take are tan but all they did was turn a ten-k run into a marathon."

She raised an eyebrow. "That was a marathon? It didn't seem that long to me."

"Brace yourself, wench. The night's still young."

I was rewarded with a mischievous grin. "You're insatiable, grandpa."

"Nay, child," I replied, taking her into my arms. I'm inspired."

We made love and slept and awoke and made love all night. At one point I awoke to find Rose standing there naked in the middle of a phone call. What I heard from my end was funny and I had to pinch myself to keep from laughing.

"...No, I'm fine....No, I have not been drinking.... Well, if you must know, I met this wonderful man...." Rose looked up at me and smiled and I realized how smitten I was already. "No, who he is, is nobody's business but ours.... No, I don't know. We just met. We really like each other.... Well, if you really must know, we're considering running off to Africa...." She winked at me when she said this and held the phone away from her ear. I could her a loud squawking from the other end. "No, of course not, I was just kidding.... Well, if you want to keep yourself up worrying, that's your issue. I'm free, single, and over twenty-one.... No, I only called so you wouldn't worry. I'm sorry I woke you up."

Rose hung up the phone forcefully. Then she walked over and kissed me gently. "That was Grace, Cody. I hoped one of the other girls would answer the phone but she's there all alone."

I nodded and held my peace, knowing I was lying with my silence. Anything I might have said could have ruined the evening and I wasn't about to risk that. What I was thinking was less than charitable. Well, that's just too damned bad for Grace. It's her own damned fault for running away. Yet as soon as the thought formed, I was glad I said nothing. Not many can stand up to a bellowing bull pawing the ground, even at three score and ten.

I should have known better. Rose had been two steps ahead of me all the way. "You were just thinking it was Grace's own fault that she's alone, weren't you?" Her eye had me penned down like a bug under a glass.

"Yes, but then I had another thought." When I told Rose what it had been she laughed.

"Yeah, you were kind of wild eyed there for a minute. When I was as young as Grace I might have run, too." I nodded and she sighed. When she looked at me I was surprised to see tears in her eyes. "We need to talk, Cody, about Grace."

"Yes, we do, but a moment of truth first. You do know that Cody Grey Adams is a pen name, don't you?"

"Yes, but it seems to fit you. At least the Cody part does." She gave me a wry grin. "The Grey does, too, gramps. Except down below. So what is your real name?" The way she asked this told me she was expecting a lie.

"My legal name is Ralph Williams. That's the one I was born with and raised. Cody Grey Adams is my registered trademark."

"What's wrong with Ralph Williams? You could use your initials if you don't like Ralph. Or call yourself Rafael if you want to be exotic." She grinned.

I grinned back. "I'd rather be erotic." Rose rolled her eyes. She was quite good at it. "The problem is that Williams is too near the end of the alphabet. Books and authors are almost always listed alphabetically. Besides my middle name is Arthur and I'm RAW enough as it is. I really don't like Rafael or Rafe, either."

There was a long silence. Neither of us was anxious to open the subject of Grace and it was Rose who spoke first. "All right, we've had our moment of truth about Cody, now what about Grace?"

"We'll get there but there's something else we need to talk about first."

Rose thought a moment, then nodded. "I think you mean contraception?"

"Yes, we need to talk about that but first things first. Is Rose your given name?"

She shook her head. "No, it's actually Rosemarie but I prefer Rose. It's simpler." Then she frowned and it was as if a black cloud enveloped the sun. "I did think about contraception at one point but by then we were already rather exposed. I didn't want to ruin the moment." I was surprised to see her blush. "Actually, the thought set off the mother of all orgasms."

"I think I know when. You really seemed to be praying a lot at one point." Rose flushed even more and wouldn't meet my gaze. "So I gather you mean we may have conceived?" She nodded. "Well, I'm sorry I didn't think of it either. For what it's worth, older men tend to fire blanks."

Rose looked up. "I hope not, Cody. I would be honored to have your child. Of course, my biological clock may have already expired. I'm thirty-eight."

"That's good," I answered. Seeing the odd look in her eyes I quickly added, "No, I didn't mean about your biological clock. I meant the age gap isn't as great. I don't feel like such a cradle-robber."

Rose came to me and took my head in her arms. I was so distracted by her wonderful breasts I almost missed what she said. "You're a good man, Ralph Williams."

I nodded. This put her left aureole in my line of sight and I gave it a gentle kiss. Rose laughed and pulled back. "You dirty old cowboy," she said, giving me a thorough kiss. "No more of that until we talk about Grace."

I nodded. "I don't expect anything will come of that, Rose."

The smile disappeared from Rose's face. "So what you said was bullshit?"

I shook my head. "Not at all, Rose. It was the absolute truth as I saw it at that moment. I meant every word of it."

"So how can you square that with us being here, doing what we're so happy doing? That feels like cheating somehow."

"One thing you need to understand is that I should have kept my damned mouth shut. What I said was an awful burden to lay on Grace. I owe her an apology. I wasn't thinking very clearly."

"Well, I can't speak for her but if you said that to me I wouldn't consider it a burden."

"Yes, Rose, but you might find it hard living up to. What I described is perfection and that is always a burden. Another way of saying it is that what I described is my dream not

Grace's. It doesn't allow her room to be whomever she is."

Rose nodded sadly. The look in her eye almost broke my heart. "I understand that but you know I can't help wishing you could say that about me, Cody."

"The difference is that with time, I could learn to love you more than I could ever love Grace." I started to say something more but stopped.

Rose caught me. "What?" I shook my head and tried to wave it off but she insisted I share it.

"It's hard to express, Rose, and I don't want to botch it. The point is that I don't know you very well as a person, but you don't seem to be afraid of the truth."

"That wasn't all, was it?" she asked.

"No, but I'm almost afraid to tell you this. One thing I really admire about you is that you aren't afraid to deflate my hubris."

Rose smiled. "Oh, is that what you call it? It doesn't seem to be that deflated at the moment, to tell you the truth. And?"

"I'm really reluctant to talk about this, Rose."

"I'm a big girl, Ralph. I can handle it."

"I certainly hope so. I hate losing two in one day."

Then it dawned on her what I was trying to tell her and Rose's eyes grew wide as a child who's seen the bogey man. "Go on," she whispered softly.

"Well, you need to understand that from all I've seen since we met, most of that profile, if not all of it, describes you to a T. My mistake was saying what I did to the wrong woman."

Rose looked like I had punched her in the gut. She grabbed me and held me close. "I just got scared, Cody," she said urgently. "I need you to hold me and let our bodies take over for a while."

I felt exhausted when we arose the next morning, totally

spent in body, mind, and spirit. I felt like I'd run a long race. It was all I could do to get out of bed and I dreaded the long trip home. Caught in a moment of madness I'd decided to drive to Austin for the book show rather than fly. Now I was faced with a twelve hundred mile drive home and I decided to stay over another day.

Rose was delighted to hear this. "It's too bad you can't stay longer, gramps. It's spring break and I have the whole week off."

"So do I. There used to be some great restaurants in town. One I remember is Mad Dog and Beans."

"It's still here. There are some other funky places if that's what you like."

"Funky's good. Tex-Mex is, too, if its not too New Age. I'm pretty traditional when it comes to food. What matters is good company." I reached out and caressed her face.

"You better watch out," she said, kissing my hand. "It's almost time to check out and you may end up paying for an extra day."

"No matter. I was thinking I could call the desk and take the room for the whole week."

"Why don't you stay at my place? My roommates are gone all week and it's not far from the University. We could walk a lot of places from there if you don't want to drive."

I glanced at my watch and reached out for her. "Checkout is not for another hour."

"Oh, no you don't," she laughed, slipping out of my grasp. I have never figured out how women do that so easily. I suppose they get lots of practice. She flipped back the covers and I discovered we'd left the air conditioner on too low.

"I get breakfast first," Rose declared. "And I'm starved. So get it in gear, ancient one."

"No respect," I replied, heading for the shower. The hot

water felt good and I was surprised when Rose joined me a moment later. "Change your mind?" I asked hopefully.

"Not for a moment," she declared and then I kissed her. My hands slipped down to grasp a wonderful gluteus in each. "On the other hand...." she murmured.

There was an IHOP on the way to Rose's place and we stopped for breakfast. We had missed dinner the night before and I ordered the whole works, artificial eggs, a full stack of harvest grain pancakes, turkey bacon and a jug of coffee. "This would be disgustingly healthy if it weren't so good," I declared when the main course was done.

"Healthy?" laughed Rose, pointing to the huge cinnamon bun smothered in butter that I was eating for desert. "I can almost hear your arteries clogging up."

She watched me scarf down the last bite of roll. When I was done, she looked at me seriously. "Ralph, we need to talk about Grace. And I'm being selfish about it, too. I don't want the situation with her overshadowing our whole week together."

"All right. I just hope we don't run into her around town. She goes to school here, doesn't she?"

"Yes, St. Edward's, and they're on break this week, too."

"Maybe we should spend the week in Cowtown," I suggested. "It's on me. I got a huge royalty check last week."

"No, it's all right. We won't run into her. We were all going to head for Galveston this week. Spring break's pretty big down there, if you like that sort of thing." She shook her head. "I don't. The only reason I was going was because everyone else was."

"Shouldn't you let them know?"

"Silly man, I did while you were sleeping. I told them I might be coming down with what's been going around." She smiled at me when she said this.

"You know, I figured out what it was I caught, the bug that's been going around."

"Oh?" she asked.

"Yeah, it's called mañanitis. You know, from mañana." Then it was my turn to smile. "Unless, of course it was the love bug, but it's been a month since Valentine's."

"Cody," she said and paused, her face a study in conflicting emotions. "Please don't push. Let's just enjoy this week we've been given. I'm not ready to go there yet."

"I wasn't talking about you," I told her. "I was talking about me and I promise not to push. Just because I feel something doesn't mean you need to feel that way."

Then I was thunder struck by a random thought. "What?" Rose asked, clearly concerned.

"I don't suppose Grace is your roommate, is she?"

Rose nodded. "Yes, she is. So is one of the other girls in the group with her. Her name is Gail but she's in Galveston, too."

"Maybe we need to reconsider going to Cowtown," I told her. "What if someone got sick and had to come home early?"

Fortunately there was no one home at Rose's place and she wasted no time packing. An hour later we were on the interstate north. Rose had parked herself in the passenger's seat and looked around my Forester with approval. "I'm impressed," she told me. "I've wanted one of these for years."

"I got it for the all-wheel drive," I told her. "It was totally practical. The roads up our way get pretty bad in the winter and we lived in the country. I got it for my wife to make it to work safely. Then after she died it became what I preferred to drive."

"When did she die, Cody?"

"Almost eight years ago. It was pancreatic cancer. The only

thing good about it was that she went fast. Six weeks after she was diagnosed I buried her." I looked at her. "Why are you impressed by the fact I drive a Forester?"

"Oh, you know. This is Texas where all the guys buy big-ass pickups with four wheel drive and brush bumpers on the front. You don't seem to have to show the world how much of a man you are by the size of your truck."

I laughed. "Believe it or not, I sold my big-assed pickup a month ago. It didn't have a brush bumper or a designer cab but it was four-wheel drive. I got it to pull our camper. We traveled a lot for a while there. I was on sabbatical and we drove all over the country."

"That sounds like fun. Did you sell the camper, too?"

I nodded. "Yeah, I just wasn't interested in camping any more after Angie died. I tried to make myself do it once, but I couldn't." I almost choked on those last words. "I'm sorry. We need to talk about something else for a while. I don't mind talking about her but sometimes it still gets me."

"I'm so sorry, Cody."

I looked at Rose and shrugged. "So, Mrs. Lincoln, aside from that, how was the play?"

Rose was not amused. "Good Lord, Cody, that was awful."

"We laugh or cry, Rose, and sometimes when we're laughing we're crying our eyes out inside. Mary Todd Lincoln went crazy, you know."

I pulled over. "I need to be quiet for a while, Rose. Would you mind taking the wheel?"

"Sure, Cody. I guess I was off base." Her eyes were troubled.

"No, not at all. You were right. It was an awful thing to say. That's one of the worst flaws in my character. I sometimes use humor to avoid pain. No, I take that back. I do it pretty often."

I leaned the seat back and closed my eyes. Then I reached

out to caress Rose's thigh. "You know, Rose, not even the President has it this good. You are a wonderful woman."

Rose said nothing but her response startled me. She reached out and caressed my cheek gently. It felt like we had been married a long, long time.

When I awoke, we were in Waco, a hundred miles north of Austin. I was surprised I slept that long and it took me a while to fully wake up. "Sorry to wake you, Cody. I needed a pit stop and we could use some gas."

"You go, I'll gas," I replied and was surprised when Rose laughed.

"It's a wonder you have any left," she said, laughing even harder at the look on my face.

I fueled the Forester and went into the station to make a pit stop myself. "Why don't we get some lunch?" I asked, pointing to a Dairy Queen a half block away.

"Well, maybe a cone or a sundae," Rose replied. "I'm still full from breakfast."

I parked the car under a big cottonwood and we brought our treats outside at a picnic table in the shade of the same tree. "All right," I said. "It's time to talk about Grace."

"What are you going to do about her?" Rose asked.

"I'm going to make amends for what I said by staying the hell out of her life," I replied. "She deserves a hell of a lot better than the likes of me."

"Stop that!" Rose answered sharply. "I'm not going to sit here and listen to you trash yourself out because you made a mistake." She smiled to take the sting out of her tone. "That only proves you're human, ancient one. It gives the rest of us room to breathe."

"Not a good idea around a gassy old goat." I replied and she giggled. "You ever met anyone who could look someone in the eye and say 'fart' with a straight face?"

Rose smiled. "That sounded like evasive humor."

"It was," I allowed. "I thought about writing Grace a letter and apologizing but I'm not sure that's a good idea. I don't know what else I can do without making things worse. I guess I could order flowers but that send the wrong message."

Rose nodded. "I think you're right. I can't think of anything, either. The best I can think of is sending a card."

I nodded and we sat there quietly for a while. Then Rose said, "You do know that she's going to write you if you don't write her, don't you?"

"Yes, but she doesn't have my address, thank God."

"As if she couldn't get it from your publisher or from the people who put on this writer's weekend," she answered.

"Well, that's a bridge I'll have to cross when need be. I think I'll probably run what I say by you first. That is, if you don't mind."

"So you're planning on staying in touch, then." There was mischief in her eyes.

"I'd sure like to," I declared. "I'd like to see a lot more of you."

Rose laughed. "You'd have to be a proctologist to do that. You've pretty much seen it all."

I reached in my pocket and pulled out a leather case. "While I'm thinking about it, here's my card." I took a pen and wrote on the back. That's my home number on the back. Please don't share that with anyone. I had to have it unlisted because of groupie calls. They seem like sweet people but they soak up hours of the time I need to spend writing."

Rose smiled. "Well, so long as they're not grope-y groupies. We didn't talk about this but I prefer to remain monogamous."

"So do I." I handed her a card with the front x-ed out.

"Would you mind giving me your phone number and a mailing address? A place I can send flowers, too."

"You're not afraid of sending the wrong message?" There was pure devilment in Rose's eyes.

"I believe I've sent it in every other way I can conceive, and maybe in that, too. I heart you, Rose."

Rose held up her hands. "More humorous countermeasures. I'm getting a little uncomfortable, Ralph." I noticed her switch between Cody and Ralph. I wondered what it meant.

I nodded. "Sorry. I didn't intend to crowd. The thing is that the further I get out on this end of life – which I hope you are able to do in good health and with good cheer – the more I understand that there are a whole lot of things which must not be left unsaid." I paused and looked at her. I was struck by how beautiful her eyes were. "That was a long complicated sentence. Did you follow it?"

"I think so."

"Let me put it another way. When you get old, death is right there staring you in the eye. You realize you don't want to leave anything important left unsaid."

Rose nodded. "That's what I thought."

"I also said that I hope you make it to old age in good health and of good cheer and that I am totally smitten."

Rose smiled. "I got that, too." An older couple walking into the Dairy Queen gave us a strange look.

"Not to be maudlin, but I won't be there to see it, at least, not with these eyes." Rose nodded, sad. "So forgive this old farter for making sure the important things do get said. And for forgetting he already said them, too," I added with a smile.

Rose smiled back. "Shouldn't that be fartist?" The man smiled as he opened the door to the dining room but the woman gave me a steely-eyed stare. I smiled at her and waved. Rose turned to see who I was waving to. The man had a hard time trying not to laugh. He gave me a thumbs-up as he followed the woman into the place, and Rose blew him a kiss.

"Now who's using evasive humor?" I replied. Rose turned back to me and looked vaguely abashed. So I continued. "The point is that I have already told you many of the things I do not want to leave unsaid between us. So I promise to try not to gush on you again."

Rose laughed and leaned over the picnic table to give me a hug. It also gave me a view I knew I would never tire of seeing. Then she whispered in my ear. "Well, I hope you gush in me a whole lot more."

The Dairy Queen had free wireless and I went to the car and retrieved my computer. "What are you doing with that?" Rose asked me.

"I'm going to make motel reservations so we have a room."

"Silly man," she replied, taking out her iPhone. By the time I had my computer set up, she was connected to the search results for motels. "Which chain?" she asked. I named a couple and told her I preferred to be on the western side of the city. I added that it needed to be La Quinta grade, or preferably better, and needed an inside swimming pool.

"You know what La Quinta means in American slang?" she asked and I shook my head. "It means next to Denny's." Then she looked at me. "I didn't pack a bathing suit."

"So we'll stop and buy you a new one." I shrugged.

Rose looked embarrassed. "I blew my budget on the writer's conference," she confessed. "I don't have enough cash with me to buy a decent suit."

I thought about this for a moment. I was pretty sure she would turn me down but I decided to take the risk. "Would it offend you if I offered to be your sugar daddy for the week?"

I asked.

Rose nodded. "I think it would bother me. A lot."

"Well, it bothers me that you don't have any mad money."

"What's that?"

"Well, my dad told me about it so the idea goes back at least to the second World War. When a woman went out on a date she always carried five or ten dollars so she could get a cab home if she got mad and walked out."

"Sounds like a good idea." I could see that this discussion troubled her.

"This is very important to me, Rose," I said. "Will you hear me out before you respond?" She was quiet for a long moment before she nodded.

"First of all, I don't like the whole idea of sugar daddy, either. So push 'pause' and erase that suggestion. However, it occurred to me earlier that if I had a medical emergency or got mugged or struck by lightning or anything else, you wouldn't have a safe way to get home. That really bothers me. I don't want to loan you the money, either. That doesn't work between friends. So I thought about it and I came up with something that might work. First of all, I'm going to ask you to hold some cash for me. It's for emergencies or serious need and I want you to carry it with you when we go out. You can give it back to me when we get back to Austin, or not. Are you comfortable with that?"

Rose nodded but she wasn't smiling. I decided to plunge on. "Just so you know, I also carry at least five hundred dollars with me when I'm traveling. It's a cash reserve and you can use that, too, if need be. As a matter of fact, use that first and don't pinch pennies. Keep the holding money in reserve to get you home."

Rose looked at me gravely. "You worry a lot, don't you, Ralph?"

"No, not really. But my writer's mind thinks up possibilities of God-awful scenarios all the time. I don't worry about things I cannot do anything about, a least I try. Yet, I try to do something about the things I can. That's what's behind the mad money thing. Once I have it covered I can let go and relax."

The older couple walked out of the Dairy Queen just then. The woman stalked straight by us, staring straight ahead, but the man turned his head and smiled. Rose gave him a full wattage smile and blew him a kiss. His smile turned into a grin and he did a couple of skip steps, waving goodbye. I don't know how she knew, but his wife turned and glared at him.

"No nooky for him tonight," Rose said softly as we watched them drive off. The idea seemed to make her very sad.

"Tonight?" I responded. "I bet it's been at least ten years since he got lucky at home."

"So why does he stay?"

I shook my head, "I've got no idea. It's hard to see how but it could be he loves her."

2

Cowtown Git-down

It was still early when we got to Fort Worth. Passing through Hillsboro we spotted a discount outlet mall and Rose was able to find a good buy on a swim suit. Even so, she refused to let me see her in it until we reached the motel. When she came out of the bathroom and modeled it for me, all I wanted to do was rip it off and have my way with her.

"Are you sure that won't get us both arrested?" I asked. It was hard to believe how beautiful she looked just then and I reached out to embrace her.

She grinned and slipped by me. "I thought you might like it, gramps. Let's swim first, while you still have the strength."

I pulled on my trunks quickly and we headed for the indoor pool. As we passed by the lobby I grabbed a visitor's guide. "We're planning on reading, are we?" Rose asked with a smirk and the desk clerk smiled.

When we got to the pool, I was surprised to see how large it was. Rose plunged right in, moving through the water like an otter, but I only stuck in a cautious toe. As I suspected, the water was much cooler than I like and I headed for the hot tub. It was free standing and large enough to accommodate a half dozen people. More important, the temperature of the water was quite warm and I sat where I could see Rose swim.

The water was warm enough I drifted off and was surprised to feel Rose shaking me. "Are you all right?" she asked, her eyes grave with concern.

"Of course," I told her and started to get up. I was surprised to find how difficult it was to stand and a little embarrassed to need Rose's help getting out of the pool. "How long was I in there?" I asked and she helped me into a poolside chair.

"Three quarters of an hour," she answered me. "I'm sorry. I lost track of the time."

"It's not your fault," I assured her. "You're my lover, not my nurse. Now help me into the shallow end of the pool. I need to cool off a bit."

I could tell Rose wanted to argue but she did as I asked. Nor did I tarry long in the main pool. When I stepped in it felt like I was stepping into a cool shower and I swam a couple of laps before I was ready to get out. By then I was beginning to feel the chill.

"You scared me, Ralph," Rose told me when we got back to the room. She was holding me tight. "For a minute I thought I'd lost you. Even though you were smiling."

I pulled back enough to caress her face. "I was? Well, I must have been thinking about you."

"Please, Ralph, I'm serious."

"I am, too, Rose. Dead serious. This is something we have to live with every day. We're never going to have decades together. Now is all we have and ten years from now I may need a nursing home. We can't change that but we can change how we live with it. And if at any point it gets to be too much for you...."

"Hush," she told me gently covering my lips with her fingers. Then she gave me an earthy smile. "Why in the world are we talking about this right now? We're all alone in a motel in Cowtown. Why don't we make believe it's our honeymoon?"

The next morning we were having breakfast and looking at the local tourist guide when Rose's phone rang. She glanced at it and frowned, then punched a button and put it away. Three minutes later it rang again. After a glance she muted the call. "It's Grace," she told me, "and she'll call back again and again until I answer. What do you want to do?"

"Find out what she wants and where she is," I replied. "I may as well take care of this today. I don't want it hanging over the rest of the week."

Sure enough, Rose's iPhone rang again a couple of minutes later. "Yes, Grace," she said, shaking her head sadly. "What do you need?" She listened a moment and then said, "Why do you want to do that? You've been looking forward to this week for months."

Rose listened for another long while and then said, "No, I don't think he was drunk... No, I didn't smell anything... Yes, I heard that, too... Yes, it was something going around... Are you sure you want to call him..? All right, I'll try to find his number. Do you want me to give him yours if I reach him..? All right, I'll give it to him and ask him to call if I can find him. Are you sure you want me to do this..? Yes, but he may not want to talk to you... Well, Grace, you didn't respond to him. You got scared and ran away."

After she said that last there was a loud squawking from her phone, so loud she had to hold it away from her ear. She spent another five minutes calming Grace down before she could ring off. When she did, Rose shook her head. "I don't ever want to do that again," she told me.

When I tried to apologize, Rose shook her head. "No, Ralph, that wasn't your fault. That's how Grace can be. I wish I hadn't said what I did. No, I wish I'd confronted her about being so childish a long time ago. She's a spoilt brat!"

"What in the world did I see in her?" I asked myself, not realizing I was giving voice to the thought.

"Do you really want me to answer that, Ralph?" Rose asked.

I shook my head. "No, sorry. I was talking to myself. I was obviously looking for what I wanted to see. I knew nothing about her." When I looked at Rose her eyes were incredibly sad. "What?" I asked.

Rose shook her head. I started to ask again but didn't. I had a pretty good idea what lay behind the look. "Did it make you wonder what I saw in you, too, Rose?" The tears running down her cheeks told me I was right.

I reached out and took her hand in both of mine. "I don't have a quick answer for that, Rose. I don't think there is one. I think the only answer will be in what you discover being with me over a long time. What I can tell you I saw was a glimpse of just how beautiful you are inside, where it counts. I hope you'll hang around long enough to see."

Rose nodded. "I will, Ralph. Now let's go back to the room and call Grace."

"I think it might be better to wait until later, after spring break. Any sooner might be suspicious."

I knew Rose disagreed but she nodded and I changed my mind. "No, I was right the first time. I don't want this hanging over us all week. What's the number?"

Making the phone call to Grace Adams was one of the most difficult things I have ever had to do. I am not sure I could have done it without Rose there to keep me honest. To tell the truth, I was hoping the call would go to voice mail. Yet it didn't and a young woman answered the phone.

"This is Cody Grey Adams," I told her. "I need to talk to Grace if she's there." Over the line I heard the sounds of the receiver being muffled and the murmur of someone talking. Yet, I could not make out the words. After that there was a prolonged silence and I considered hanging up. Had Rose not been there I am sure I would have, even knowing that would make things worse.

Then another voice came on the line. "Yes?" it asked and I had no idea who it was. I had never heard Grace's voice except when she was screaming at Rose over the phone.

"I need to talk to Grace Adams," I said, feeling totally foolish.

"This is she," the voice told me.

"I believe you were at the writer's conference this last weekend, weren't you? The one in Austin."

"That's right," the voice told me. I wondered why Grace was making this so difficult. Then I realized she was scared.

"I believe I owe you an apology," I replied. "Your roommate gave me this number. I seem to have let my mouth run off ahead of my brain."

"Yes, you scared me." The fear I heard a moment before seemed to be abating.

"I understand that. I can be rather intense and you have my profound apologies. How can I make things right?"

"You can start by telling me the truth," she said. I could hear her fear giving way to umbrage. "Did you really mean what you said, Cody?"

"I did at that moment. Then I realized later how unfair it was to dump my feelings on you the way I did. I truly regret not keeping my thoughts to myself."

"How do I know you mean you say right now? How can I trust you?" The way Grace said this sounded like it was right out of a soap opera script.

"You can look at the truth in what I do. I meant it when I asked how I can set things right."

"And how do you intend to do that?" Grace demanded.

"The only way I know is begging your pardon and staying out of your life."

"So you can just tell me you're so sorry and go on your

merry way?"

I have experienced many arctic blizzards living where I do in the northwestern reaches of Minnesota. Yet none of them were as cold as those words. I had to make a conscious decision at that moment to stick with the conversation. It was tempting to simply disconnect.

"You know, Grace, this whole conversation seems to underline just how wrong I was, doesn't it? I really don't know you very well. Can't I at least plea temporary insanity?"

Again there was a long silence but I waited patiently. She'd had time to brood over her hurt and nurse it. What she said next made it clear she had no intention of letting it go and moving on to better things. "You're kind of late saying you're sorry," she said. "Why didn't you apologize the next day?"

"I was indisposed that evening and the next day," I temporized. "I spent them in bed." Rose rolled her eyes when I said this.

"Well, what about since then? That was a long time ago."

"I think if you think about it you'll see it's only been a couple of days. Three as a matter of fact." I was stretching it allowing her that many.

"Couldn't you have called sooner?" It was clear she was not about to let me off the hook.

"To be honest, I didn't have the number and I was ashamed of making such a fool of myself. I truly didn't want to make things worse." Again there was a long frosty silence and I decided I had enough. "Look, Grace, either accept my apology or not. I hope for your sake you do. Either that or tell me what more I can do to set things right. I'm willing to do what I can but I'm not going to play this kind of game."

Grace replied by slamming down the receiver. "That went well, didn't it?" I said, looking at Rose. Then another thought struck me. "Do you think Grace is aware of you and me?"

"She may have put two and two together. When she called me yesterday she was really nosy about what I'm doing."

"I didn't realize that was her calling. I thought it was a nosy friend or roommate..." I stopped, then added, "Which is exactly what it was. Sorry, I didn't intend to eavesdrop."

Rose smiled. "You didn't but thank you for the apology. I don't think Grace is exactly a friend, either." She shrugged. "At least, I doubt she will be when she finds out about us. On the other hand, it's no big loss."

"Talk about being totally wrong!" I said still not believing the phone conversation I just had. "Or did I just bring out the worst in her?" Rose shrugged but said nothing. "How could I have been so wrong?" I asked myself once again.

"Are you asking for an answer?" Rose responded. She seemed troubled. "Are you sure you want one from me?"

"Please. I don't understand what just happened."

Rose sighed. "The kindest way of saying it is that you weren't looking at the flesh and blood Grace. Think about it, Ralph. You'd just been Cody Grey Adams the famous writer talking to your audience about your deepest desire for a soul-mate. I imagine a big part of this has to do with losing your wife. The point is, you had incredible rapport with your audience and you opened yourself up to us. You had us captivated, completely in your hands. And you were...well, drunk, for lack of a better word, drunk on our adoration. We gave you a standing ovation, but then it was over and you began to crash...."

Rose stopped and looked at me with a terrible desolation. "Are you sure you want me to go on, Ralph? You may find what I have to say rather painful."

"Please, Rose. Just tell me the truth."

Rose sighed. "All right then, Ralph. You were totally into Cody mode when you came out of the conference room.

Ralph was wherever he goes when Cody is doing his thing. Cody was drunk with the wine of our adoration, but even more he was drunk with the wine of his desire for the woman of his dreams. Are you with me so far?"

I nodded and a cold hand of dread clutched my heart as Rose went on. "You told us this was the woman you had dreamed of finding all your life, and you told us all about her. There was not a woman in that room that didn't wish it was her. Then it was over and I think you must have felt very sad, almost crushed, maybe."

I nodded dumbly. "Then when Cody saw Grace, there was something about her that coincided with his ideal well enough he could force it on her, make it fit. And he did it in a way that few woman could resist."

"I just spoke the truth as I felt it," I objected.

"Yes, I know you did. I saw it and it was terrifying."

"Terrifying? How?"

Rose looked into my eyes deeply, then nodded. "Maybe it's a gender thing. What I saw looked like Romeo all rolled up into Rambo running rampant. Have you seen any of those old paintings about the rape of the Sabine women?"

I nodded. I had seen more than one and they were awful. While the artwork in all of them was incredible, I had never understood why anyone would choose to paint that scene. At best it was well executed pornography. Rose must have seen something of this in my eyes because she touched my cheek gently. "And you did it so sweetly there was not a woman in that hallway that didn't want to be ravaged. By you."

I shook my head. "I still don't understand why she's so bent out of shape."

Rose rolled her eyes and threw up her hands imploring the heavens. "Cody, you told her she was the one! You injected a big dose of romance into her life she had never experienced, and may never have even dreamed she would have. Then you didn't do anything about it."

"How could I? She took off and left me there looking like an adolescent with a boner."

"You didn't pursue her! Now she's had time to dream of Prince Cody taking her away from her excruciatingly boring life. Now you call and tell her it was a false alarm. How in the world did you think she would feel?"

I sighed and shook my head. "Are we good? You and me?"

"Of course we are," Rose said. "Why wouldn't we be?"

"You just demonstrated what a blind dumb-shit I can be," I told her. "It's hard to imagine you would even like me after seeing me the way you described."

Rose cuddled my head between her lovely breasts. "Oh, Ralph. Don't you understand? That's the way Grace looks at things. I don't, not for a minute. All that shows me is that you're human. As I said, it gives me room to breathe."

"Would you hold me for a while?" I asked. "I'm feeling a little shattered." When she started unbuttoning my shirt, I added, "I just want to cuddle. At least for a while."

"I know," she murmured as she stripped off my clothes. "But I like the feel of your skin next to mine." Then she giggled. "Am I supposed to ignore that reflex?"

It took us a couple of days before we managed to get away from the motel. There was a Mexican restaurant next door where we took most of our meals and the motel provided a Continental breakfast that included waffles and fruit. We spent a lot of time in the indoor pool, too, talking when we weren't in the water. I was careful how long I lingered in the hot tub and I noticed Rose checking the time, too.

"Is this a honeymoon?" I asked at one point as we sat by the pool, taking Rose completely off guard. A symphony of feelings played across her face, surprise, hope, joy, and not a little fear. It took her a long moment to recover. "I was just teasing, Cody," she replied. "I said we could pretend."

"So what would be different if we weren't?" I asked. "Would you call me Ralph?"

"Don't toy with me, Cody," she said, looking at me gravely.

I got the point immediately. "This is Ralph asking, my love, not Cody. I'm not playing with you."

"I know. You just startled me. You can be pretty intense." She looked down, then raised her eyes to mine. "The truth is I was just then wondering the same thing. I was thinking how hard it's going to be when you get tired of me." Seeing the shock in my eyes, she added gently, "Well, you did ask."

"Good Lord, woman, look at us," I told her. "Here you have an aging Falstaff in all his rotund glory and there you sit in that suit, turning every head that walks by. Who do you really think is going to tire of whom?"

"Well, Sir John, at least you use correct English." There was a devilish gleam in her eye. "That's got to count for something. On the other hand, I think Ralph is kind of cute."

"You never answered my question," I persisted. "And Ralph is the English teacher, not Cody."

"I know and I'm not going to," she riposted. "So there!" she declared, sticking out her tongue at me.

"So Italian is all right for supper, then?" I asked innocently.

Rose was startled once again. "How do you do that?"

"What do you mean?" I replied, knowing full well what she was asking. When she me a stern look, I relented. "I pay attention," I added. "I saw you looking at that Olive Garden ad in the tourist guide. I thought if I fed you I might get lucky."

I was surprised when this brought tears to her eyes. "Oh, Ralph," she said, reaching out and touching my cheek tenderly. "You don't have a clue, do you?"

I had no idea what she was referring to or trying to tell me but I new better than ask. "I guess not." I paused, at a loss for words then said, "Well, how about them Vikings?"

"What?" she laughed. "You mean the football team? What does that have to do with anything?"

"Absolutely nothing," I assured her. "That's just what Minnesotans say when they can't think of anything else."

For some reason that tickled her and she began laughing, normally at first but then so hard it scared me. Not knowing what else to do, I picked her up and tottered into the pool. This set off even more laughter and then to intense horse play that ended in a kiss.

This, of course, led to other things and we beat a hasty retreat to our room. As we were lying quietly snuggled together in the aftermath and I was nodding off, I heard Rose giggle. I was too far gone to speak but grunted something like "urg?" To which my lovely companion snickered again and murmured, "How about them Vikings?"

The next morning I awoke early and made our first cups of coffee from the complimentary service in the room. The smell of it brewing awoke Rose and I kissed her. Then I waited until she had drunk half her cup before asking if there was something special she would like to do or see.

"I don't know," she said when I asked. "I never spent much time in Fort Worth. Maybe the water gardens. I saw that in the tourist guide. It looks interesting. What are my choices?"

"Well, we're not far from the Fort Worth Zoo, which is well worth going to see. There aren't many cages except for the birds and during the week it shouldn't be crowded. Not far from there is the Japanese Zen garden, which I really like, and not far from that is the Kimball Art Museum.

There's a Salvatore Dali exhibit going on there if you like his work. Going downtown there is the water park complex you mentioned and Tandy center. Tonight there's always Billy Bob's if you like country dancing. There's lots of other stuff, too."

"The zoo sounds like fun," she told me. "So does the water park and I'd like to see the Kimball, too. I've heard a lot about that. I'm not much into country music but I do like line dance. How about you?"

"I'd really like to see the Dali exhibit, but not everyone likes him. I could stop by on my way home from Austin if you don't care for him. I'd also like to visit the Zen garden. I've never seen it in the spring." With someone I love, I thought to myself but was careful not to say it. I must have expressed the thought somehow because Rose smiled at me gratefully. She seemed able to read me like a book and that wasn't an altogether comfortable thought. Not even Angela had been able to read me this clearly.

"That must be a terrible gift," I observed and she was clearly taken aback. "Or is it just with me?"

"You have no idea," she told me softly, shaking her head. It was quite clear she didn't want to talk about this. Yet, I was wrong. "Sometimes it's so painful I can hardly look."

I let it go then, but I wondered. It took me a while putting pieces together, but I finally figured it out. What Rose could see so clearly in other people was how they felt, not the day-to-day details of their lives. Yet she also had a keen eye for detail when she chose to focus her attention, not unlike Sir Arthur's famous detective. So what appeared to be mind reading was a highly intuitive reading of how the pieces of any given human puzzle fit together. The reason she was able to read me so well, besides the two of us being so much alike, was because I had her full attention.

We had a leisurely breakfast and decided to go to the water gardens first and the Kimball after lunch. When we got to the water gardens Rose was particularly taken with the active pool, and when we had walked down to the bottom of the steps she looked around, puzzled. "This feels so strange. It looks familiar but I've never been here before. I don't think I've seen it in a magazine or on TV, either."

I chuckled and Rose looked at me, frowning. "What's so funny?" she demanded.

"That's the same reaction I had when I first came here," I told her. "Do you read or watch much science fiction?"

"No, not much. Star Wars and Star Trek are about all. Some of the classic movies, too, maybe but not the horror stuff like Alien or The Blob. Why?"

"There was a science fiction movie back in the mid 'seventies that won all kinds of awards for special effects. It was called Logan's Run and Michael York played the lead. Does that sound familiar?"

"No, not really. Michael York sounds vaguely familiar. Why?"

"Well, some of the best scenes in the movie were filmed right here in the water park. Look it up on Google. We can watch it tonight when we get back to our room if you want."

Rose nodded vaguely and it was like a cloud blocking out the sunshine. "Do you mind sitting here for a while?" she asked. "This is really nice." Then she smiled and took my hand, sitting close, and the sun came out again.

As I sat there in the sunlight of her smile, I wondered what it would be like spending the rest of my life in her company. So I closed my eyes and allowed myself to go with the flow of that question. I thought what it would be like discovering the many things that made her who she was.

I suspected that life with her would always be intense, and that even fighting with her would be as intense as the way we made love.

Knowing myself, I hoped I would always measure up. So I made a solemn pact with myself to do everything I could to be the man she needed me to be and I directed a request to Whomever it might concern for the grace to do that. This surprised me since I am not a religious soul.

What startled me even more was the clear sense I had been heard. There was no burning bush, no chariot of fire, nor even a small still voice speaking within my mind. There was only that clear sense my prayer had been heard.

I was startled by herself gently nudging me in the ribs. "Are you in there, Ralph?" she asked. Seeing she had my full attention, she asked, "Where did you go just then?"

I was surprised at her question, that she even had to ask. "How long was I gone?"

"At least fifteen minutes. That's when I looked at my watch. You looked so happy I hated to disturb you but I got scared. You didn't seem to be breathing at one point."

"I was in a very happy place," I told her. "I still am, being here with you."

"Would you mind telling me what was going through your mind?"

"No, but it might scare you. So maybe we need to wait for a while and just enjoy the day. I will say I was day dreaming and you were very much part of it."

Just then my legs reminded me I had been sitting in one position too long. "I need to stretch," I said, and started to get up. When I did, I almost fell into the large pool at the very bottom of the steps. Had not Rose not grabbed me I think I would have fallen. My knees seemed to have turned to rubber.

"Thank you," I told her. "Seems like grandpa's stiff in all the wrong places." I began flexing my legs to work out the kinks but the result was a painful tingling.

"More defensive humor?" Rose asked.

"No, Rose. I'm just trying to stay on the sunny side of the street. Had I fallen in and drowned, I would have died a happy man. Thanks entirely to you."

"And I would have had to watch you die," she reminded me.

"I'm afraid that's inevitable. I'll do all I can to make it worth your while. That's how it was with Angela, my wife. Even the worst days were good. I'd gladly do it all over again, even knowing how it would end."

"Well, you may have to if we decide to stay together. You could outlive me, you know."

I shook my head. "No, you're not allowed to die first. That's part of the deal. Now let's try to get me up again. I have an urgent call from Mother Nature. All this rushing water doesn't help a bit."

When I got to my feet a lady sitting on the next step gave us an odd look. Seeing her expression I realized the sound of the water had not masked our private conversation. So I smiled and shrugged, and kissed my companion lightly on the lips, and the lady looked away. I could tell Rose had seen all this, too, and was amused.

The tingling was abating and this time I was able to move my legs more or less normally. Even so, I took it easy going up the steps. As I did I felt Rose's presence behind me all the way, ready to grab me if I stumbled.

"Now let me show you my favorite part," I said when we got to the top of the active pool.

"I thought you had, several times," she answered, laughing, giving me a gentle push toward the men's room. Then she ducked into the ladies' side.

When I came out Rose was already there and I pointed toward the stairs leading down to the Meditation Pool. "That's my favorite part of the park," I told her. "The reflecting pool. The steps over here are smaller and a lot easier to climb. There's even a ramp for us ancient ones."

When we got to the top of the stairs Rose reached out and took my hand, intertwining her fingers with mine. It was a very intimate thing but I knew it was partly to catch me if I fell. I had to remind myself this grew out of her caring for me and I raised her hand to my lips and kissed it.

As I had hoped, Rose was quite taken with the quiet beauty of the tall cypress growing around the pool. "Oh, look at the little people!" she said, pointing at the cypress knees growing around the tall, elegant trees, delighted as a child. "I wish I had a real camera," she told me, pulling out her iPhone and snapping a couple of shots.

"You can use mine," I said, pulling a pocket sized point-and-shoot out of my photo vest.

"You have lunch in there, too?" she asked, taking the camera. She had teased me about the vest when we left the motel. "Are those your zoo rags, grandpa, or are we going on safari?"

"Can't be too prepared for Cowtown," I had answered. "You never know when you might run into a buffalo or something." The truth was that I always carried several high energy bars in the vest along with a pack of trail mix for munching. It was one of those things I did so I didn't have to worry about finding a place to eat. When we stopped at a discount store the day before I had stocked up for two.

"How do you work this thing?" Rose asked me. She had already found the power button and was trying to find the view finder.

"It's called point-and-shoot," I told her dryly. This earned me a head shake and eye roll. "It's fully automatic but you can fool with the zoom if you want. It's on top next to the shutter button. Use the screen on the back to frame your shots. Just like your iPhone."

"How many pictures can I take?" She was looking at me and pushing the shutter.

"As many as you want. The card holds several hundred."

Rose nodded and turned back to a group of cypress people in a spot the sun shone through. She began to work her way around the group and I was struck how methodical she was. I said something about it and she turned back to me and smiled. "Photography 101," she told me, turning back to her subject and moving on around the tree.

"My turn," I said when she handed back my camera. She tried to protest when I turned it toward her, but I insisted. "Think about us making love," I told her and I was able to catch the instant she blushed. I was also able to catch several more wonderful shots of her expression. It was a wonderful sequence going from mild embarrassment to profound desire and it gave me some of the very best images I've ever captured.

Just then I heard someone asking softly, "Excuse me, please. May I get by?"

I moved aside and turned my head. When I did I saw it was the same lady from the active pool. My camera was still raised chin high and on impulse I pushed the shutter, unintentionally catching a burst of three images. When we looked at them on my computer later, I was surprised how clear every one of them were. Yet it was the lady's expression that caught my attention. She was looking directly at the camera and her face filled the frame. What I saw there was heart breaking. It was an intense study in the loss and grief

I knew so well. The tears in the lady's eyes were quite clear.

"How long was she there?" I asked Rose.

"A couple of minutes, at least," Rose told me. "She was coming toward us when I handed you the camera and she stopped when you stepped back."

"So she heard what I said to you," I replied.

"I don't see how she could not have. You were speaking a bit loud. I could hear you quite clearly."

"I was speaking up so you could hear me over the sound of the water," I said. "I was having trouble hearing."

Rose smiled and chuckled. "The people on the other side of the pool weren't. They turned to see what was going on." Then she laughed. "You're blushing!"

"You don't know what was going through my mind just then." I told her exactly what that had been.

"Well, you don't know what was going through mine," she replied. "It was exactly the same thing. Only it was me doing it. I got so hot I thought I was going to faint."

"Well, maybe we need to do something about that," I said, seeing the look on her face.

"Maybe we do," she responded softly, tearing at the buttons on my shirt.

It was later that afternoon, when we were quietly snuggling in one another's arms, that I remembered something I wanted to say. "You know, Rose, you have a very good eye for photography."

"That's what my instructor told me," she said. "I got the highest grade in the class. What's strange is that I had never used a camera before that class. I seemed to instinctively know what to do to get the best shot. It was so easy I almost took the advanced course, too. My teacher encouraged me to do so but it didn't make much sense at the time. I didn't need the credits. Why, do you think I should?"

"I can't say whether you should or not. You're the only one who can decide that. What I can tell you is that you seem to have a very good eye for it. You made the little cypress people seem like they were alive. It looked like they were on their way somewhere, as if they were about to jump out of the planting bed and head out."

"That's how they felt to me," she answered. "If you think about it they are alive, Ralph. They are part of the tree. I think I was just picking up on the life force inside them."

"The Force?" I smiled. "I think it's more than that. I think you could go to a field of dried up rocks and make them seem alive. No, it's more than that. You could bring them to life."

"That's only because they are alive, Ralph. All I do is to catch that when I see it."

"It's more than that, Rose. You seem to know exactly what to do. You make good use of the Rule of Thirds and you have a good sense for mood and light. The shots you took today make it look like the cypress people were on the move."

"Yes, I know that but I can't begin to do what you did to get that woman's face the way you did."

"That was pure serendipity," I argued. "A happy accident."

"I think the polite term for that is horse apples," Rose said with a smile. "You saw something that was there and gone in an instant and your finger pushed the button at that exact time. Getting three shots rather than one may have been an accident, but the first one is the best. Chance had little to do with it."

I shrugged. "No, Rose, I lucked out, believe me. Most of the pictures I shoot like that don't turn out well at all. I have no idea why I pushed the shutter right then."

"Training," she told me. "You didn't have to stop and figure out what to do. You just did it. Just like a pro."

"I'm an amateur," I insisted.

"Right, just like Blakely Hunt." Seeing my surprise, she laughed. "He's one of my favorite people. I've never met him but I know a lot about him. His work is incredible and he's won all kinds of awards. He won the National Geographic photographer of the year award several years ago, but you'll never guess who was his first runner up. That's right, folks, it was another amateur, an unknown photographer from northern Minnesota who didn't even use his real name."

She had me dead to rights. "Don't believe everything you turn up on Wikipedia," I told her. "The name could be pure coincidence."

Rose hooted. "Balderdash!" Somehow she made this sound more obscene than its original dysphemism. "How many people in the United States do you think are named Cody Grey Adams, Ralph? Damned few."

One thing age can teach is when one is on the losing side of an argument. "Thank God for that!" I said and Rose smiled. I really liked the fact she didn't rub it in and told her so. "As a matter of fact, I seem to be liking more of you every day," I told her. Her lovely breast was hanging just above my left eye and I turned and kissed it gently. "You're beautiful," I murmured. "Is it too soon us use the L-word? That seems to be very much on my mind at the moment."

"Is that what you call it?" she grinned, giving me a gentle squeeze. "Mister L, as in Long?"

"Or L as in Lazarus, rising from the dead. Or maybe as in Lover or...."

She raised a hand and touched my lips. "We've only known each other less than a week, Ralph. Please don't push."

"I was actually going to add 'Like' or 'Lust.' I know you need time, Rose, and I didn't mean to push. Please, just ignore me."

"Now how am I going to do that?" She snickered, glancing down at my response. "Are you going to feed me, Master, or are you intending to starve me into submission?"

"How do you feel about fish?" I asked. "I was thinking of Pappadeaux."

3

Theophany

An hour later we were having coffee after a sumptuous feast of New Orleans creole gumbo, secret recipe hushpuppies and a wonderful coleslaw the waiter assured us was made fresh on the premises every morning. As good as the food was, it was the ambiance that impressed me the most. No mater how often I visit one of the Pappas restaurants, I have the sense of eating in a family establishment. I think that's one of the key things that makes them so popular.

As we dined, we talked about our afternoon. We had ended up staying much longer than we intended at the water gardens, mostly sitting and talking the way new lovers do. Our lunch was late, power bars from my vest and soft drinks from a street vendor. While the food in the cart smelled delicious, neither of us cared for the look of the vendor or his stand. His hands were dirty and the cart looked like a breeding ground for ptomaine, so we both settled for canned pop.

Our drinks were not exactly cold, either, which seemed to confirm our suspicion of tainted food. "It makes you wonder how they get past the health inspectors," Rose pointed out.

"The power of green miniatures," I told her.

"Green miniatures?"

"Yes. Benjamin Franklin and Ulysses Grant are very popular these days. Hamilton and Jackson just don't make it, and neither does Thomas Jefferson. Grover Cleveland and William McKinley bring more but are hard to find."

"What in the world are you talking about?" Rose

demanded. There was an edge to her voice.

"Filthy lucre!" I declared. "Moolah! Cash money. The root of all evil."

"I might have known!" Rose replied, looking at me askance. "Are we anywhere near Sundance Plaza?"

"Maybe a mile," I told her. "It's probably less from where we parked. Why?"

"I was reading about it in the visitor's guide. I want to see the Kennedy memorial there. Are you up to the walk?"

"Sure," I told her. "Which way?"

Rose pointed out the route on our visitor's map and we set off, passing in front of the huge Convention Center. We had only walked a block or so when Rose said, "Look, there's Saint Patrick's Cathedral. Do you mind going in? I'd like to see it."

"Sure," I said. "I don't think I've ever been there."

While I am not high on church, I have visited a number of large churches around the country. My interest is mostly architecture, atmosphere, and stained glass. The newer ones leave me unmoved, coming across like large decorated boxes. Yet the older ones rarely fail to touch me, even the simplest country chapels, and some of them are quite remarkable.

I remember the first time I visited the north star cathedral in Saint Paul. From the moment I entered I was enveloped by an overwhelming sense of benevolent presence. This became even stronger as I moved into the nave and it never left me as I moved around the building, looking at the side altars and the windows and the statues. I stayed there a long while and when I left, I had walked away with a sense of sadness that I could not remain longer. It was clear to me that Someone or Something not of this world dwelt there and delighted in my presence.

I have experienced this in a number of older churches

and I have no rational explanation why this is. Yet the older I get the more attuned I seem to be to this experience and I was not surprised to feel the same when we entered Saint Patrick's. Someone was very much at home there and I knew I was very welcome. What came to the mind was the prodigal son coming home to a father delighting in his return.

One thing that surprised me was when Rose dipped her hand into the font of holy water beside the entrance to the nave and crossed herself. Not knowing why, I did the same. It felt odd doing this but the numinous presence did not seem displeased and I wondered once again why I felt so moved. There was nothing in my background to explain it and I was startled to feel tears flowing down my cheeks

I decided not to resist but to accept this for the gift it was. When I glanced toward Rose she was watching me intently. She looked happier than I had ever seen her and I could see tears in her eyes, too. Then she came to where I was standing and took my hand, leading me into an alcove. This one was dominated by a pieta similar to Michael Angelo's original in Rome. To one side was a candle stand with four rows of long burning blue votives and it was clear even to my uneducated eye that this was a place reserved for quiet prayer and contemplation.

One of the areas where I part ways with the Roman church is in the quality of contemporary artwork and design. Though I am a confirmed agnostic, I am also very much a traditionalist when it comes to sacred art. This may or may not be a bit hypocritical since I am not a player, but for me the purpose of art is to touch us where we live. Done right, artwork slips around the defenses of our thinking minds and confronts us with the terrible beauty of human life and existence. Nor does it give answers, but done right, it raises questions we need to ask. Even more, it demands a response from us even if this is only an acceptance of life on life's demanding terms.

The paradox and the mystery I find in doing this is that I am able to live at peace with myself and with others in a very troubled world. I am able to live with the terrible loss of the wonderful gifts we are given and I am able to do this without resenting their loss. The flower blooms and then fades and dies, bringing forth a promise of new life in the seed it produces. Great art somehow helps me accept this and not lose hope for redemption of the common grief I share with every human being on this earth.

The point is that tacky church art grates on my soul like fingernails on a chalkboard. There is no excuse for it in my mind and it tempts me to resent the artist for inflicting such poor taste on the world. Not to mention resenting the purchaser for settling for cheap and for encouraging such hideous work by actually buying it.

Even so, the pieta I saw in Fort Worth was not cheap. It was well done but it did not touch me in the way the original in Saint Peter's Basilica did when I first saw it. To be honest, back then the original did not affect me the way such things do these days. As a young man I was far too angry for that. Yet it left a mark that remains after more than fifty years. I was in the presence of the original less than a minute, but I still remember how it felt to touch the foot of the madonna smoothed by the touch of five centuries of pilgrims.

As a man grown old I can still see in my mind's eye the stain my young eyes saw, the stain that countless human fingers left on the stone as they sought the gift of their hearts' deepest desire, the gift of grace and hope in a world gone mad. Somehow the sight of this had left a deep impression in my soul fifty years before, one I tried to deny and even to exorcise. Yet the tears flowing down my cheeks that very afternoon told me I had failed. They told me that Someone or Something had listened to the deepest longing of my soul rather than the raging insanity of my mind. For that I found myself very grateful.

I tried to explain this to Rose when she asked me about my experience that afternoon. Yet when I was done, she looked as puzzled as before. "Let me write it out," I told her. "I do my best thinking at a keyboard." She smiled when I added, "Or with a number two yellow pencil."

"Does it have to be yellow?" she asked with an impish grin.

"No, as a matter of fact. It actually flows better with a high quality ballpoint. It's like a dialogue with myself but I don't have to worry about grammar or spelling or even complete sentences. I use a lot of dashes and when I'm done I can usually understand what I meant to say."

"What if you can't?"

"That works, too. Sometimes my reconstruction is a whole lot better than the original idea."

"Why use a keyboard then?"

"I can correct as I go," I told her. "Sometimes when I am typing out the body of my sketches I get bored and have to push myself to finish."

"Could it be because what you think needs to be written is boring?"

"Ooh! You don't pull punches, do you?" I said, clutching my midriff.

Rose held up her hands. "I'm sorry. That didn't come out the way I meant it."

"Actually, I think it did, but that's all right. I know you're not a slasher, Rose. The truth is I figured it out a long time ago. When I'm feeling boring, I'm probably being a bore. And if what I am writing bores me, it's damned sure going to bore a reader. Seems obvious, doesn't it?"

Our conversation moved on to our visit to Sundance Square. I had not seen the area since it had changed hands and had been renovated to became City Place. Nor was what I remembered that fresh in my mind. What I could recall was looking down from the scariest escalator ride I had ever taken and wondering how in the world I was ever going to make it down. That image imprinted itself on my soul. Yet I could not remember if I ever rode the Tandy Center Subway. It ran between the shopping mall and the parking area some distance away. So I must have taken it but I simply could not remember. From the pictures I've seen it looks vaguely familiar, but who knows?

"The only time I ever visited Tandy Center was after the mall was going downhill," I told Rose. "I can't even remember why I went there or even if I had company. I just remember getting on this very narrow escalator that looked way too flimsy to support its own weight."

"Then I looked down at the ice rink. All I could see around me was glass walls and the escalator down on the opposite side of this huge empty area and I could almost feel myself falling all the way down to the ice. SPLAT! I don't even remember what was at the top of the escalator – unmarked offices, I think – or how I ever got back down. It must have been on the escalator but I simply can't remember."

Our visit to the JFK memorial at Sundance Square was interesting but nothing to write home about. Looking over the transcript of John Kennedy's off-the-cuff remarks I was not particularly impressed. Yes, it was impromptu and the man was laying a foundation for his political agenda in the coming election. Yet somehow the rest of his remarks did not live up to his opening words, "There are no faint hearts in Fort Worth." Given the crowd, who had waited patiently in the rain to hear him, I think he would have been cheered for simply raising a fist and declaring, 'Cowtown forever!'"

"So what do you think of him as a man?" Rose asked as we drank our final cup of tea after dessert.

"He was very charismatic. Looking back now, I think he was far more effective as a martyr than as a President. Not that I wanted him dead. He was a personal hero and I was just as devastated and just as angry as anyone when he was killed. Maybe more. Even so, his death brought Lyndon Johnson to power and LBJ knew where the bodies were buried. He was a master wheeler-dealer who knew how to get things done, and he pushed every major piece of social legislation that Kennedy had put on the table through Congress. The only major mistake that Johnson made was over Vietnam. Kennedy had not yet made up his mind about that."

Rose nodded. "That seems to be the consensus from what I've read. Vietnam almost destroyed the United States."

"Yes, but it went much deeper than Vietnam. That was only a focal point. The underlying issues LBJ inherited went all the way back to our colonial period, if not before. They were the same issues that led to the Civil War. They have never been resolved and we will have to keep dealing with them over and over until they are. At least, that's what I think. We don't seem to listen to each other or learn from our mistakes."

After dinner we drove around for a while before we went back to our room. By the time we got there I was having a hard time staying awake. Between the food and the exercise we got walking around downtown I could barely get myself undressed. Rose was glad to help but it didn't do her much good. I dropped off the moment my head hit the pillow.

Even so, there are some benefits from having to get up for a pit stop in the night. I was not even half awake the first time and Rose let me be. The second time, however, she was on me like a panther when my butt hit the sheets and she had her way with me thoroughly.

"Tell me in the morning," I mumbled as I was drifting off once more.

"Tell you what?" Rose whispered back, wide awake.

"Tell me how much I enjoyed it," I managed to respond. I do remember her laughing. Then I was gone.

The next morning it was sprinkling and we decided to tour the Kimball Art Museum first. I was just as glad. My aging frame was still creaking from the day before and I was happy to be able to meander from one thing to the next. Rose didn't care much for Dali but she insisted on going to the museum. "I'm sure there's plenty of other things for me to see," she said. "Maybe I'll see something of Dali's I'll like. Things look different in photos."

I couldn't argue with that. As a young man I had seen Rembrandt's Night Watch at the museum in Amsterdam. It covered an entire wall, roughly twelve feet by fourteen and it was impressive. The people in the foreground appeared to be life sized and the perspective worked incredibly well. There was no question in my mind why this was called a masterpiece.

Even so, just before I turned the corner to see the Rembrandt my eye had been caught by another painting. To this day I don't know who the artist was who painted the pastoral scene that captivated me so completely. The canvas must have measured about three feet by four, but what captured my attention was the artist's mastery of light. Somehow he had captured the incredible beauty of an overwhelming golden light I have seen only a few times at sunset. At that moment it seemed like I was looking through a window into another time and another place. Even more, the light called to me, inviting me to step through that open window and become part of that time and place.

Compared to what I had just experienced, the Night Watch was a disappointment. It was excellent work and no doubt a real masterpiece. Yet it did not call to me. It did not invite me into its time and place. What it did was to illuminate the stern faces in the foreground and to give a sense of strong character and resolve. What I was being given was a glimpse into their world, but the looks of the men's faces told me there was no place for me there. It was as if a line had been drawn at the margin of the image, a line that told me not to move closer.

I had never really thought about this before and it was very much on my mind on the way to the Kimball. When we got there the museum wasn't open yet. There was a small queue of early birds standing by the doors and I parked where we could watch the entrance from the car.

Rose asked where I was, I told her what I had been thinking. "One of the things I like about Dali is that I've never felt excluded by his work. It's like he simply presents what has come to his mind as he was working and invites me to come in if I dare."

"If you dare? That's an interesting way of putting it. Do you think of it as a challenge?"

"No, not in any personal way. Salvatore Dali was confrontational but that was the way he met the world. It's just that I find some of the images he presents very disturbing. At least, I did when I first started looking at his work. The older I get the less I do."

"Why do you suppose that is?"

"I seem to have learned a thing or two. A long time ago a man I studied introduced me to a simple thought. He wrote something to the effect that it is a basic spiritual truth that every time we get upset, no matter what the apparent reason may be, the source of our upset is us. Those were not his exact words but that's the gist."

"I'm not sure I agree with that," Rose said. "There are lots of people in this world who didn't choose to be the victims the way they were made to be. Particularly children."

I nodded. "Yes, but he was talking about adults. I think he would have made an exception for very young children. Older ones are like everyone else, they have a hand in making the troubles they find. They start testing the limits very early."

"I don't know. It seems to me that spiritual axiom flies in the face of human experience."

"Well, I hated the idea. There was no question about that. It was only when I made it personal that it made sense to me."

"What do you mean?"

"Try changing 'I' to 'me.' Then it reads that any time I am disturbed, no matter what the cause, there is something wrong with me. To put it another way, aside from the child abuse I experienced, my troubles have been of my own making. Every time I have been disturbed as an adult, I had a part in setting things in motion. I think the cause of my troubles is my own pig-headed self will."

"What about when your wife died? You didn't cause her cancer, did you?"

"No, I didn't, but I didn't handle her death very well at all, either. I did some very destructive things, Rose. Fortunately, they were mostly self-destructive but I caused other people grief, too. It was understandable and I was doing the very best with what I had to work with, but that wasn't very damned good. Not at all. I don't resent myself for it any more but I wish I could have done better. It's like the thing with Grace. I could have done better. I could have kept my mouth shut."

"Well, from a selfish point of view, I'm glad you didn't. If you remember, that's what brought us together. Cody was in a lot of pain, Ralph."

"Most of which he created for himself. God, it's hard being human!"

Rose nodded and thought for a moment. "So what does this have to do with Dali, with your not finding his images as disturbing as you first did?"

"One way of saying it is that I've become comfortable with my own subconscious. The things I see there are not so scary any more. They are simply things I need to know and I work at trying to honor and understand them. The challenge is in decoding what they mean. With Dali, his images are from his unconscious. They are not attached to me the way my own are. So if I don't fear my own, why should I fear his?"

Rose nodded. "That makes sense." Then she pointed. "Look, they're opening the doors."

Part of the joy I find visiting the Kimball is that the building that houses the Museum of Modern Art is itself a work of art. Each piece on exhibit has ample space to be appreciated for its own merits and this allows viewing any particular piece from a lot of different perspectives. This makes a difference in what I see and sometimes the artist is very playful in choosing the angle that gives the truest view of the work. At times they also play with different views and Dali does this. Look at one of his works from one angle and you will see one thing. Look at it from another and you will see something else.

That morning I was delighted to discover that the focus of the exhibit would be on the sculpture of Salvatore Dali. These are not as well known as his paintings and many people seem to think of Dali as only a painter. The images they seem to remember best are things like his warped clocks in The

Persistence of Memory, or the surreal Sacrament of the Last Supper, or maybe the suspended crucifix of Christ of St. John of the Cross. All those are powerful images.

What is sometimes forgotten is the fact he was also a master sculptor. The challenge that a sculptor faces that a painter does not is that sculpture is art in the round. Every perspective is critical and this lends a power to the work that a painting often lacks. Yet it can also be a distraction. The melting clocks appear in his sculpture, too, but these don't seem to have the same elegance or precision as those in his paintings. Some of the perspectives don't work as well, either.

Even so, I was like a kid in a candy store, wanting to taste it all. It was hard to focus on one piece, to contemplate it with my full attention. When I tried I was aware of everything I had not yet seen, and this almost had a disastrous result.

Even though the focus was on Dali's sculpture, the exhibition also included some of my favorite paintings of his. I had never had an opportunity to see any of these in person and when I rounded the end of a display partition two of them were hung on the opposite wall. I was drawn to them like a magnet and I didn't notice the other works in that area. Seeing the two of them side by side was incredible and began to I move around, trying to find the best angle to view them.

I have no idea why I stopped when I did or why I turned around at that particular moment. Yet when I did, there I was, face to face with Dali's Crucifix of St John of the Cross not four feet away at eye level. I felt like I had been punched in the solar plexus. I had never been so close to anything radiating as much power as the elegant brutality of that simple figure. The feeling was so strong I backed up a step and could do nothing but stand and stare as tears streamed down my face.

I must have gasped because Rose was suddenly there by my side, holding my arm. I think I might have fallen had she not. I was grateful for her presence and even more grateful that she said nothing. When I thought about it later I was most grateful I had not blundered into the crucifix and knocked it over.

I took a while for me to regain my composure. When I did I began to move around the statue, absorbing it from every side. It was only about eighteen inches high and set at just the right height for viewing. The details were an effective mixture of abstract detail and stark reality, and they were as equally well done in back as in front. Later I learned it was cast in bronze but in the light of the gallery it seemed as if the head and shoulders had been done in silver.

I don't remember anything else of that visit except that Rose was by my side with every step. I do remember asking her to drive us back to the motel and to order take-out if she wanted lunch. I vaguely remember her undressing me and getting me into bed, and she was there when I awoke much later.

"How do you feel?" she asked, clearly concerned.

"Well, I've never run a marathon but it felt like I might have just done so emotionally. Other than that, I feel fine." Then I saw the clock. "Good Lord, did I sleep all afternoon?"

"Yes, I was beginning to get pretty worried. Your pulse was good and so was your breathing, but I was about to take you to the emergency room, anyway. You slept over three hours."

"I think I need a shower," I told her. I had on a tee and shorts and I began taking them off. When I did, Rose began to undress, too. "You planning to jump me in the shower?" I asked. The sight of her lovely skin was delightful.

"You should be so lucky, Ralph" she snorted. "I'm planning

on keeping you from falling and busting your ass."

"That's good. I'm not sure how much good I could do you, anyway," I replied.

"Right," she said, glancing down.

When I followed her gaze I was surprised to see myself aroused. "My goodness," I told her. "It would be a shame to waste that."

I opened my arms and she came into them. She hugged me tightly and then burst into tears. "Oh, Ralph, I was so scared," she told me when the storm had passed.

I sighed. "Twice in one day is not good," I agreed. "Are you sure you want to hang out with this old codger?"

Rose pulled back. There was fire in her eyes. "You dumb shit!" she declared, roughly shoving me back onto the bed. She was on me like a cat on a rat, straddling me and pinning my arms over my head. Then she showed me how intense it could be like making up with her.

When she was done instructing me Rose looked into my eyes gravely. "Damn it, Ralph," she declared. "Don't you understand? I'm falling in love with you. God help us, but I am. It scares me."

There was a great vulnerability in her eyes when she said this. So I kissed her lightly on the lips. "At the risk of pissing you off, I am, too. We need to talk about this, but not right now. Right now I need a shower and a good meal."

Things were different between us after that, even better somehow. Yet, we didn't have much of the week left. That night was Thursday and we had been lovers for six days. I needed to be home on Monday for classes and it was a two day drive from Austin. There wasn't much time left for us. "I'm trying to figure out logistics," I told Rose over supper, explaining my schedule. "I can get my TA to cover my Monday classes but there's a faculty meeting I need to attend on Tuesday."

There were tears in Rose's eyes when she replied. "It's going to be awful saying goodbye, Ralph. I miss you already."

"I know. I'm trying not to think about that. I wish you could come with me. Is there any way you could?"

"You know how to tempt a girl," she replied. Then she giggled. "What would your cohorts say if you show up with some floozy from Texas?"

"Woman," I told her. "You're about to piss me off, calling yourself a floozy."

"You don't know my history, Ralph," she said. "Not that there's anything that bad back there but you don't know that. I haven't murdered anyone or been busted for drugs, but I could have. Are you comfortable with my word about it?"

"Yes, I am," I responded. "I seem to be a fairly good judge of character and I trust that. On the other hand, you don't know my history, either. Maybe we need to put that to rest by having it checked out. Would that help? We could do it online but it might better to use a standard service."

"I hate this," Rose told me. "We need to trust each other for this to work."

"I agree. On the other hand, I would feel better with you knowing there is nothing back there."

Rose nodded. "That makes sense. What do we need to do?"

"We need to exchange our full birth names, date of birth, and Social Security numbers. That's a major leap of faith in itself, trusting each other with our identities. Then we each ask a professional to run the check."

"I wouldn't know where to start finding a professional, one I could trust."

"Ask your insurance agent," I suggested.

"I don't have an insurance agent," she replied.

"Don't you have to have car insurance in Texas?"

"I don't have a car, Ralph. I've got a garage but not a car."

"How do you get around?"

"I catch rides and take the bus or ride my bike. One of my roommates will usually take me for grocery shopping and stuff like that. Or one of my friends."

"Sounds like you live pretty close to the edge, Rose. Do you mind my asking how come?"

"School. I pay cash and carry and I don't have student loans. So I have to be very frugal. I don't smoke or drink, either. That helps."

"What's holding you in Austin?" I asked. "Classes?"

"Not really. I'm finishing up my thesis right now. My research is done except for last minute things. I have until the end of the summer to complete that and submit the first draft."

"Yeah? What's your major?"

"English. Modern American writers." Rose seemed troubled by the question.

"Ah, so you were checking one out at the conference. Or am I full of myself?"

Rose blushed. "Busted. It gets worse." I couldn't understand the fear in her eyes. "I never meant to get involved, Ralph. You were there and so I was, to get to know you and your work better. And then...you know how it just happened."

I could feel my mood sinking but didn't know why. "What are you trying to tell me, my love?" I asked gently.

"My specialty is modern American romance writers. One of the writers I'm looking at is a very private fellow from northern Minnesota."

Rose looked like she expected me to kick her and I couldn't figure out why. "So who are you looking at? Nerburn?"

"No, Ralph. I've been looking at Adams." She wouldn't

meet my gaze and her face was stricken with shame.

I was stunned. I thought she had been teasing. "You've got to be kidding me."

"I'm afraid not. Now I've got to throw everything out." She began to cry. "I'm sorry, Ralph."

I was having trouble getting my soul around this and I was at a loss for words. "Please say something, Ralph. I know it looks awful but I didn't set out to seduce you."

It was then the implications hit me. "I'm a bit overwhelmed, Rose," I answered. "I need to be alone for a while." I handed her the keys to the Forester. "I'll get a taxi back to the motel. I just need some time to walk and think."

Then something else crossed my mind. "Why do you have to throw everything out?"

"Because I don't want to lose you, Ralph. I love you and it's not worth risking that." She reached out and touched my arm. "Please give me another chance."

I looked at her and saw nothing but goodness. I couldn't believe I had been that blind. "You haven't done anything wrong, Rose," I told her. "You've been very kind and very generous to an old man and I'm flattered. I've just had one of those days and I'm on overload. I need to sort things out. I'm very tired."

I started to leave and then turned back. "You can use anything you've learned over the last few days. So don't throw anything out. It would trouble me to no end if you did." I gave her a gentle kiss on the lips. "I'll be all right. So don't worry."

I woke up in a hospital bed. There was a crucifix on the wall facing my bed. When I turned my head there was a clock on the other. It told me the time was 6:34. The light coming in the narrow window told me it was morning. There was a plastic ID band on my left arm and I saw a call button strapped to the crib bar intended to keep me from rolling out of bed.

I pushed the call button. When someone answered I asked where I was. I was told someone would be down to see me. I asked them to make it quick. I needed a pit stop and preferred to have someone to make sure I didn't fall.

Someone turned out to be a pleasant looking nurse. She was delayed, however, and the call of nature got pretty severe. So I tottered into the rest room and was dressing myself when she arrived. "What are you doing?" she asked.

"Oh, I'm getting dressed. I thought that would be better than walking around town in a hospital gown. Where am I? It looks like I'm still in Cowtown."

"You're in Saint Elizabeth Seton hospital," she told me. "You were found unconscious last night in the chapel of Saint Patrick Cathedral. No one could wake you. You did come to for a few moments at one point and asked us to call someone named Rose. Then you lapsed back into a coma again and no one could wake you."

"So what did you all do with me?"

"Your vitals were all good so we put you in a bed for observation. We did take a blood sample and an EKG to see what might be the cause. Your blood alcohol level was very low and nothing else showed up on the EKG. You're scheduled for a CT scan and a neurology consult this morning."

"Well, those will have to wait until I get home to Mayo's. At the moment I need breakfast and a phone. I assume you gathered all my valuables and locked them up."

"You can't leave," the nurse protested. "You might keel over in the parking lot."

"I won't be driving," I told her. "And you apparently didn't find anything wrong with me. So I'm leaving. Where do you have my valuables?"

We went back and forth for a while about that and one of the administrators even showed up. Yet there was no legal reason they could keep me. So I was released AMA after I was able to give my correct name and date of birth and signed a quitclaim. They wanted to know my Social Security number, too, but I pointed out that they had no need of that and I paid my bill with plastic. They did make a copy of my driver's license and group health card, but I refused to show them my Medicare card. As everyone and his brother knows, the first eight digits of your Medicare number is your Social Security number.

There was a pay phone in the lobby and the first thing I did was to call the motel. Yet there was no answer from our room when I asked for it. When I called again and talked to the clerk, he told me Rose had left about a half hour before. The motel had received a call from the hospital and the clerk had passed it along to our room.

I wondered how the hospital knew where to call. Then I realized I had a plastic key card in my pocket with the name of the place on it. Fortunately, Rose had reserved the place in my personal name, not my pen name, and the hospital people had pulled my information up of my driver's license. This was not exactly kosher, as I pointed out to them, but I let it go. God and the nuns can teach a Missouri mule a few things about being stubborn.

I took out my cell phone and tried to look up Rose's number but it was not among my contacts. Then I realized I had written it down but had forgotten to punch it into my phone. Nor was the scrap of paper I had used in my wallet. Galloping senility, I scolded myself. You're ready for the nursing home.

A calmer part of my mind told me to chill out. It reminded

me that things tend to turn out all right and that I'd been very lucky to be found by a sexton rather than a mugger. As an afterthought, I did direct a plea for help toward the heavens for Rose and I to reconnect as quickly as possible. Then I had to laugh. No sooner had I sent the message than I turned around and saw Rose coming in the main doors.

When Rose spotted me she ran to meet me and threw herself into my arms. "I was so worried," she told me. "Then I got all pissed off. Then I got worried again. Thank God you're all right! What happened?"

"I'll tell you over breakfast," I told her. "We may as well eat here. I'm starving."

"How did you wind up here?" Rose wanted to know.

I told her what the nurse had said. "I don't know how I got to the Cathedral," I told her. "My feet and legs are a pretty sore so I must have walked."

"That's five miles, Ralph! You could have been run over!"

"Old writers never die," I told her. "They just smell that way." I regretted it the moment the words left my mouth and raised my hands. "I know, Rose. Deflective humor. I'm trying to break the habit."

Rose smiled at me sweetly and reached over and pinched my leg, hard! "That's how I'm going to help you, sweet man. Every time you do it."

"That's elder abuse," I protested and she smiled sweetly and did it again. "And that's for walking off and leaving me high and dry," she added. Then the tears came. "God, Ralph, I was so scared."

"At the risk of getting pinched," I replied, "There is a silver lining. How shameless are you?"

"When it comes to you, I'm way out there. Obviously. Here I am shacked up with you in Cowtown, USA. What's the silver lining?"

"Well, if you can stand my company a little longer, I have an excellent medical reason to stay in Fort Worth for a while. After all, I almost collapsed twice yesterday and I did end up in the hospital this morning. I also seem to be experiencing retrograde amnesia. It doesn't particularly scare me but I do think I need to get it checked out. Here in the city I'm surrounded by competent medicine."

Rose looked at me. "Well, it scares the shit out of me," she said, clearly angry. "I'm not pissed at you. I'm pissed at God for letting it happen. Not that it's any of my business. That pisses me off even more."

"Rose, you are the woman of my dreams, the woman I love more than life itself. As far as I'm concerned, it is your business if you want it to be. But try to look at it this way. Maybe this is a wake-up call from Whomever is in charge. Not just to me but to you, too. Maybe we're being given a reason to be more mindful of how we live."

There were fresh tears in Rose's eyes when I stopped. "Would you like to live with me for the next couple of months in Cowtown?" I asked.

"What about your job? You're expected back next week."

"I will be taking emergency leave to get this checked out. Between what happened last night and what happened at the Kimball, it's pretty obvious what I need to do. I have a great TA and the university can get along fine without me until next fall. But I do need an answer from you. I can stay here and check this out or I can risk driving home. But I will not stay here alone. Is it too soon?"

Rose took a deep breath. "Damn you, Ralph. Why do you have to be so sweet?" she growled. "I could probably tell Cody to stick it where the sun don't shine but I don't have much defense against Ralph. How would we do this?"

"I think it would be best to stay in Forth Worth," I told

her. "I could come down to Austin, I guess, but I think that would look a little suspicious. Since it happened here, I think I need to get it checked out here. You would be free to come and go as you please if you need to get back to Austin for a few days."

"I don't have a car, Ralph."

"Of course, you do," I told her. "You could use the Forester or we could find you what you like. I'm not talking about a Lexus or a BMW but what I got for my big-ass truck would cover a new Legacy."

"You know what I'm afraid of, Cody? I'm afraid I'm going to wake up and find out this is all a dream."

I leaned forward and smiled, patting her hand. Then I pinched her leg, but not as hard as she had pinched me. "Hey!" she said, indignant.

"Sauce for the goose," I told her. "I guess you're not asleep, are you?"

"That's even scarier."

My conversation with the Dean went well. "I was lucky it happened here in Forth Worth," I told him. "I can't imagine what it would have been like if I'd been driving through rural Oklahoma."

"That would have been a nightmare," he said. "I think it would be wise to have it checked out there. Any idea how long that might be?"

"At the very least, I'd say a couple of weeks," I replied. "The doctors here were stumped. On the other hand, it could drag out like it did when Angie was sick. So I think you better prepare for it being through the end of the semester. I can email lesson plans and exam questions for my TA, and papers can be emailed directly to me down here. Everything's digital these days so it shouldn't be a problem. I could even tape lectures and send those. I've got my computer with me."

"No, I think you need to concentrate on getting well," the Dean told me. "We'll give your TA an assistant to take care of some of the scut work. So don't worry about things up here. But keep me posted how things are going. Do you need us to send anything your way?"

"No, I've got a manuscript on my laptop to keep my mind occupied. It needs a lot of revision but there's no deadline, thank God. At least the writer's conference is behind me."

"Well, maybe you should consider finally retiring," the Dean said lightly. "You've certainly earned it. We need to give the young Turks a chance."

"I thought we had with you, Chuck," I quipped and the Dean laughed. I had been on the committee who hired him fifteen years back.

The next call was to the doctor who had treated me at the hospital. When I explained what I would like to do he was very encouraging. "I think you're very wise to do this, Doctor Williams. Or is it Adams?"

"It's Williams, Doctor," I replied. "Adams is my trademark. Is there any reason we cannot do this on an outpatient basis?"

"No, not as long as you follow our protocols. You will need someone to drive you here and back. It takes several hours for the medications to clear your system and it's not safe to drive. Do you have a personal physician?" I told him I was hoping he might make a referral and he gave me three names. "Ann Smith is the sharpest of the three, but you didn't hear that from me."

"Hear what?" I asked and he laughed.

After I hung up I called the hospital doctor's schedule nurse and set up an appointment for the next day. The purpose was to explain the protocols for me and to answer any questions I might have. Then I called Rose to let her know I was done and when we needed to be at the hospital the next day. She had been out looking at furnished apartments and had a couple for me to look at that afternoon. "But only if you feel like it," she added. "The doctor told you to take it easy."

"When I was a kid we used to say we'd take it any way we could get it," I told her. "How about a late lunch?"

While I was waiting for Rose I called Ann Smith's office and explained the situation. The secretary put me directly through to the doctor and we visited briefly. We arranged for me to come by the office that afternoon to take care of paperwork and when I hung up I understood why the doctor at the hospital spoke so highly of her.

Rose was in much better spirits when she arrived back at the motel a little after one, and she was full of energy. "Thank you," she told me over lunch. "I haven't had this much fun in ages. You were right about using a property management agency. The thing is, everyone wants at least a six month lease."

"I have an idea," I told.

"You always have an idea, ancient one."

"Now that you mention it, I have several," I told her, wiggling my eyebrows like Groucho Marx. "One is about our options and we have several. Have you ever considered living in a nice hotel? It might be the cheapest way."

"Why don't we let that one bake a little longer?" she replied.

"All right. A second is to rent an unfurnished apartment with just a refrigerator and stove. I think we need three bedrooms so each of us has a place to work."

"So what are we going to sit on?" she asked. "Besides our duffs?"

"Well, we could make a run by Ikea and pay them to deliver what we buy. Then, when we are done in town, we can simply sell the stuff or give it to Good Will."

"Or we could rent furniture," she said. "That sounds better."

"Yes, but that's not much different from renting furnished. I would prefer to have our own new mattress. You know, so we can raise our own bedbugs."

She nodded, smiling. "Inherited ones are so tacky. All those stains."

"Or we could buy a motorhome and become trailer trash."

"Careful, Cody. That slur is a little close to home." Seeing my look, she relented. "It's all right. You didn't know. Just be careful with the aspersions."

"Is that one of those special forks you use for asparagus?"

"Now that one was not bad."

"There's something you need to now, Rose. Two of my favorite folk were an aunt and uncle on my dad's side of the family. They were trailer people. They followed road construction and raised several kids in a twenty-five foot trailer. When my uncle retired they parked it and built a house around it. But they always lived mostly in the trailer. They were the most generous people I've ever known."

"How in the world did they have the privacy to conceive the last two or three?"

I laughed. "I wondered that, myself, but I didn't ask."

"Don't ask, don't tell," Rose murmured, giving me a look that was impossible to mistake. "You know, Ralph, all this talk about conception has got me all riled up."

"Goodness," I murmured back. "Maybe we need to do something about that. Let's go plant a baby."

"Please don't joke about that, husband."

"Husband?" I asked. "When did this happen?"

"Don't get all excited. I'm just trying it on for size."

"I've got something else that needs trying for size."

"Well, let's go see if it measures up. Or is it down?"

"No, it's around and around in the mulberry bush."
"You're terrible, and, yes, I do like it."

4

Down Home Texas

Rose and Doctor Ann, as she preferred to be called, bonded immediately. The good doctor was very direct with us, starting with the nature of our relationship. I jumped in quickly.

"We haven't discussed it but I'd like Rose to have my medical power of attorney." I told her. "I don't have siblings or living children. My late wife died from cancer several years ago and my daughter and son were killed in a car crash a couple of years before she died. Our only grandchild died in the collision, too."

The doctor nodded. "So how long have you two been together?" she asked.

"A week," I replied and the doctor blinked.

"She's the woman of my dreams," I explained. "I have been writing about her for thirty years." I smiled at Rose. "I've been looking for her even longer."

The doctor looked at Rose, who was blushing. "Neither of us have anyone else, doctor," Rose said. "I've studied Ralph's work for several years. I've researched him thoroughly."

"She means she's studied Cody," I clarified. "That's my pen name, Cody Grey Adams. I'm a teacher and a writer."

"*Midlife Crazy*," the doctor said. "I've read it. It's a rather unusual love story. Wasn't there a writer's conference recently?"

"Last week," Rose replied. "That's where we met in person."

"Now here you are in Fort Worth," the doctor said, shaking her head. "Where is home for you, Ralph?"

Northwestern Minnesota," I answered. "Rose is a graduate student at UT Austin."

The doctor looked at Rose. "So you've been in infatuated with Cody for a long time."

This was a statement, not a question, but Rose nodded. "Not like I am today," she said simply with a smile that melted my heart.

The doctor nodded. "Well, I'm sure you are both aware of the issues you're up against. At least there are not children involved."

"At this point," I interjected.

"I lost a child several years ago," Rose told us. There were tears in her eyes. "It was at sixteen weeks. His father punched me in the stomach. He was drunk."

"Did you prosecute?" the doctor asked.

"Yes, but we weren't married," Rose answered. "So the judge threw the book at him. He's still in prison and I've been very careful ever since."

"With contraception?" the doctor asked.

"Avoiding exposure. Except for Ralph. My roommates call me Sister Rose." She was smiling and looking directly at me when she said this.

The doctor looked at me and Rose told me later that I was grinning like an idiot. "This is apparently new information but I gather you're not displeased by it, Ralph. Am I right?"

"Yes, but we have talked about it," I told the doctor. "After we had been exposed, but if Rose is with child, who better than the mother of my child to make bottom line decisions? The overriding point is that we don't have decades, Rose and I. We have today and if you all find out something is wrong with me, there's an even greater urgency."

As we walked out of the doctor's building we decided to have lunch at the restaurant next door. When we came in I was amused to see a discreet dress code notice by the maitre d'hotel station. A waiter appeared out of nowhere and led us to a table, asking what we would like to drink. While we were waiting for our drinks, I looked at the menu. The prices marked the place as posh but then the really posh places don't price the menus.

"You know, Rose," I said once we ordered. "A whole lot of things would get a lot simpler if we just got married. I'm not pushing but it's true."

Rose looked at me gravely. "Some other things could get a whole lot more complicated if we did," she replied.

"Could or would?" I asked.

She smiled. "Could. I won't be owned by anyone, Ralph. As much as I love you, that does include you."

"I would never presume to try to own you, Rose. I can't imagine anything which would sour what we have more quickly. What I am most concerned about is protecting you and whomever might be residing in your womb." Seeing the look in her eye I held up my hands and added, "Yes, I know you can protect yourself quite well, thank you very much. But what I can give you is leverage. Is that wrong?"

"No, not a bit." She looked up at me and smiled. There was a mischievous gleam in her eye. "You know, Cody," she added, emphasizing my pen name, if you proposed to me right this moment and I accepted, Ralph would wet his pants."

"You're probably right. So would you. What do I need to do, bellow and snort and paw the ground?"

"Now that might be fun, right here in front of God and all these people." Yet when I started to stand up, she became alarmed. "No, Ralph, I was just kidding."

The couple at the next table were trying hard to pretend they hadn't heard us. Then the woman snickered, trying to pretend it was a sneeze, and we all broke up. "My granddaughter and I are the early floor show today," I told them and turned my attention to my love. She was having a hard time containing her laughter, too.

"Is everything all right, sir?" another voice asked. I was amazed how much disapproval the head waiter was able to load in those five words.

"We're fine," I told him. "It was the pepper in their salad." I nodded toward the table next to us.

The woman at the next table sorted and broke out laughing. Her companion looked like he was having convulsions and knocked over his iced tea. This set all of us off again and it was all I could do to keep a straight face. "The gentleman may need some iced tea," I told the head waiter.

By this time everyone in the place was watching and some kind soul started clapping. This turned into a round of applause and the head waiter flushed. He snapped his fingers at a couple of waiters watching and stalked off. A moment later our waiter brought the man next to us more tea. Seeing the mess on his table I invited them to join us and the waiter waved up a helper and they joined us. The switch was smooth and done in half a minute.

I introduced us to the couple, who turned out to be named Gay and Guy. "I don't want to be nosy, "Gay asked. "But we couldn't help hearing everything you said. Are you all a couple?"

"We're trying hard to be," I told them. "We haven't known each other very long, so it's an interesting process."

"How long have you been together?" the woman asked.

"Almost a week now," Rose told her.

"And you're already talking marriage?" the man inquired.

"Yes," I told him. "She's the woman of my dreams."

"They do it all the time on TV," Gay chipped in. "What's

the name of that show? You know, the one where the bride and the groom meet for the first time at the wedding."

"Marriage at First Sight," I offered and Rose gave me an odd look. I shrugged. "The department secretary is seriously addicted to it."

"The department?" Guy asked." Are you a policeman?" I wondered what was behind the look of fear in his eyes.

"No, I'm a simple college teacher," I answered and saw fear displaced with a heart breaking relief. "An English teacher."

My confession of being a college professor led to a wandering discussion about fiction and creative nonfiction, and what I was doing in Cowtown. "I'm on the way back to Minnesota from Austin," I told them, knowing this would lead to even more questions. I was right and we spent a good while answering the standard questions people ask successful writers. I have been tempted to write these down in a FAQ brochure I could hand inquisitors. This would probably not do much good since most people seem to prefer being told something rather than reading about it.

"I don't want to be rude," Rose broke in smoothly after a while. "But Ralph and I have an appointment across town in less than thirty minutes. So we better go."

I was amused by the ease Guy had letting me pay the tab for us all. I assured him that I, after all, was responsible for spilling his tea and he went along with that canard.

"God, I thought we'd never get away from them!" Rose told me as she wove our way through the afternoon traffic, scaring me to death with every lane change. I had to work hard restraining my brake foot from trying to find the pedal. "Why do they need to know all that?"

"Short answer?" I said and she nodded. "Their lives are dull and boring. You and I are a hot item for their gossip circles."

"I hate it but I think you're right. How sad."

"Opinion?" I asked and she nodded again. "I think that's why so many people in the country are so angry all the time. The so-called American Dream has failed for them. At least, it's failed to make them feel good about themselves. They've acquired all the stuff but they sense this gaping emptiness inside themselves and can't find anything to fill it. That's a twenty-first century take on quiet desperation."

Rose nodded. "You know, I remember reading that back when I first read *Walden*. What got to me was the comment about the despair that lurks under what we call games and amusement. For a while that was a real wet blanket for me. I found it hard to enjoy the things I always had. Then one day I got mad. I told brother Henry David to take a flying leap at a rolling donut. I was going to enjoy what I took joy doing."

"Good for you! I think brother Dave was looking in a mirror without knowing it, not through a magnifying glass. It's deceptive and a lot of good writers make that mistake. For some reason they believe their opinions are gospel truth, implanted at conception. They seem to not understand how their mind-set clouds their perception."

"Present company excepted, of course."

I had to smile at that one. "Of course," I agreed. "Always. It amazes me how few writers realize that what they are really writing about is themselves. It's risky to generalize from a universe of one. That's misleading to your readers more often than not. It all starts with self-deception."

"So much for no man being an island."

"No, not at all. It's like there is a competitive drive to be unique and it's as if some people try to make islands of themselves by pointing out how they are different. The reality is that there is a whole world of common ground lurking beneath those differences. John Donne was right."

"I wish I had a tape of you just then. You looked like a fired-up preacher-man exhorting the choir."

"Ooh! That bad, was it?"

"No," she replied. "It was kind of hot to tell you the truth. I see why people like revivals."

I laughed. "My dad used to say there were a lot babies conceived at those, not all of them in holy wedlock."

Rose nodded absently. "Do you remember when Thoreau wrote *Walden?*" she asked.

"It was before the Civil War. Somewhere around 1850, maybe a little later."

Rose nodded and was silent for a while. Then she looked at me and said, "Do you know what really scares me, Ralph?"

I shook my head and she continued, tears in her eyes. "I'm caught in a real bind. I hate the thought of losing you. Yet I also hate the thought of hanging on so hard it smothers you and drives you away. I hate the thought of us ever falling out of love with each other."

"Not going to happen," I said with resolve. Seeing my eyes go wide with fright, she looked at the road and narrowly evaded a major crash with two semis. "Is my driving bothering you?" she asked, looking back at me.

"Of course not," I answered, patting my clothes. "I seem to have lost my rosary." She thought that was funny.

"Are you Catholic?" Rose asked one day out of the blue. It was a couple of weeks later and we were lounging around our new apartment waiting for the dray service to deliver some furniture. I detest the smell and weight of particle board, as does Rose, I discovered. So we had looked around and were very lucky finding an upscale used furniture place. It was well stocked with wooden furniture that had been finished but never painted. While this meant very little of our furniture matched any given style, we managed to put together a harmonious mix of similar pieces. Rose called the style Late Graduate School.

"No," I answered her question. "I am a true agnostic. Why do you ask?"

"Well, you crossed yourself with holy water at the cathedral and you had a very strong reaction to the crucifix at the art museum. You also mentioned your rosary the other day."

"I was just joking about the rosary. The people around here drive like kamikazes." Including my beloved, I thought.

"You mean I do," she grinned.

"I'm going to plead the Fifth on that one. To answer your first question, I find catholicism attractive, especially the spirituality of things like the mass and the rosary. The Church itself is intolerable. It seems to me they put a great deal of effort into controlling people's lives. Crossing myself with holy water was a first, by the way. The reason I crossed myself was because you did."

"No, that's not completely true," I told her. I explained my sense of Presence in certain places. "It was my way of honoring Whomever dwells there, too. It's sort of like bowing to traditional Japanese or saying 'namaste' to traditional Indians."

"What about the crucifix?"

"That was gut wrenching. Dali's crucifix is the most powerful art I have ever seen, but it doesn't have the same power in a photo or picture. I have no idea what my response was all about but it went to the center of the emptiness I carry inside me. It reminded me forcefully that there is nothing on this earth that will fill this emptiness, not even church. Or, maybe, especially not church as most people seem to understand it. If I were a religious person, I would say that the hand of God touched me."

"So what do you say as an agnostic?"

"Not to be trite but I'd say Whomever seems to dwell in the cathedral moved me in a way nothing ever has before." I shrugged. "That's the best I can do. I'm still trying to get my mind around it."

"Maybe that's not the right part of you."

"I don't understand. What are you saying?"

"Ralph, you're an academic, a scholar. You live in your head, in a world of ideas. Maybe it's your heart that needs to grow around the experience."

Before I could answer she shook her head. "Wait. That's not quite right, either. Maybe you need to allow your heart to grow around it. I think that may be what you want."

When Rose said this I felt a benevolent warmth surround me. I recognized it as the same Presence I encountered in Saint Patrick's. I also realized it was no accident that I had ended up back at Saint Patrick's that night. Or with Rose as my companion.

I must have been quiet for a long time. It was only when Rose touched my face that I became aware of this world again. She was looking at me, alarmed, and I realized my face was wet with tears. "I'm all right," I assured her, reaching out and taking her in my arms. "My world just got turned upside down again. It seems to happen pretty often these days."

Rose didn't answer. She simply held me close. "I don't know why this is happening to me right now," I added. "Maybe I have a tumor."

My beloved shook her head. "No, they would have found it already. The doctor told us that, remember? Where did you go just then? When you checked out."

"I have no idea. Wherever it was, I knew I was safe and that I was loved." I smiled. "I almost hate to tell you this, but I also knew you were absolutely right. It's my heart that needs to grow. The thing is, I don't know how to let it."

"I don't know, either, Ralph. Maybe it's too simple minded to say this but maybe you need to ask for help."

It was a couple of weeks after that we came as close to a real fight as we ever had before. Rose needed to go back to Austin to see her advisor and I insisted we get her a car. I tried every argument I could think of but she wasn't buying.

"You can help me with plane fare and cabs," she declared.

"Will you at least come looking with me?" I asked. "Would that hurt?"

Rose's answer was a stubborn glare that could have curdled milk and it was apparent I was barking up the wrong tree. So I played what I figured was my high card. "Damn it, woman, if nothing else would you please take the Forester?"

"I'll take cabs. Or rent a car. And what if I wreck the Forester? Have you thought about that?"

"It's insured. You're already on my policy." I had done this at the doctor's suggestion that Rose do all the driving. She made it quite clear that she did not want me behind the wheel until she and the other doctors thought it safe. This was not just for me, either, but for other drivers. A couple days before our conversation they had told me I was well enough to drive again. Yet Rose still did most of it. Aside from all the near misses, I learned that I loved having a chauffeur. It was a real gift.

Even so, adding Rose to my driving insurance had been a bit strange. For one thing, I learned that I had never asked her full name. When we signed the leasing agreement for the apartment I assumed she used my surname to avoid questions. Then I asked for her driver's license to tell my agent the number and did a double take. The surname on the laminated card was exactly the same as mine. "I wondered how long it was going to take you to ask," she laughed, seeing my response. "For the record, that is my birth name, my dad's name."

"So you never married?" I asked. She looked so sad when I said this I was sorry I asked.

"No, I had three near misses," she told me. "The first was with a guy who eloped with one of my friends. She paid for it, though. He turned out to be a real rat."

I tried to apologize for asking but Rose waved it off. "No, Ralph, it's all right. You need to know. I missed a world of heartache with that asshole. The second time was the guy who beat me and killed our child. The third time it was simply sad. We lived together for four years and were going to get married, but we never got around to it. He was a professional fireman and was killed fighting a warehouse blaze. That was two years ago and what I regret most is that we never had children. We were going to but...." She began to cry and I had held her a long time.

As usual, Rose smelled a rat in the woodpile when I insisted that she take the Forester to Austin. "You're up to something, Ralph. I can tell." When I rolled my eyes and threw up my hands she laughed. "You do that well," she said.

"That's my line," I said. "I've been taking lessons from you."

It took some discussion but Rose finally agreed that it made more sense for her to drive the Subaru than dealing with taxis or a rental car. The cost of additional insurance was a large factor in her decision. Yet she was still very reluctant to take the cash I offered. "Look, we're living together and we're sharing a bed," I pointed out. "We also led the property manager to believe we are husband and wife. You've been taking care of me and getting me where I need to be, and you're my medical decision maker if I cannot make them myself. We even have the same last name, for goodness sake. A good case could be made that we are, in fact, already married."

"Yes, but I haven't consented to marriage yet," Rose pointed out. "You may already be my husband in my heart, Ralph, but I want a real wedding. I've never had one."

"Then when it's time, we'll have one, complete with marriage license, mariachis, and all." I hesitated, then said, "Not to probe a sore point but do you still have the mad money I gave you? You'll need some for food and gas and I'd feel better knowing you have a reserve."

"I still have it all," she replied and I gave her three hundred more. "This is for travel expenses and incidentals and I really don't want to argue." I gave her a stern look and she laughed. I rushed on before she could disagree. "Any idea where you might stay?"

"I thought at my apartment. That means putting up with Grace but at least it's paid for. It's walking distance from where I need to go and there's a garage for the car."

"Not so loud or she'll hear you," I whispered. "She's a Forester, an SUV. Nobody ever told her she's a car." My reward for that one was another eye roll and a head shake. That led to other things and we took a long time with our goodbye. By then it was well into the afternoon and Rose decided to wait until morning. "Good," I told her. "I miss you already."

She nodded. "I miss you, too. This is the first time we will have been apart since we met," she pointed out. "That's been over a month. It might be good for us, you know. You've been restless the last few days."

I nodded. "I've been cooped up too long. I need to wander around with the camera and stretch my legs. Spring has sprung and all that. Maybe I'll visit the Zen garden or the zoo."

"Spring has sprung and all the rosebuds are blooming in tight shorts and tighter tees," Rose observed dryly. "Just watch your step with strange women, Bud." It was the first time I had seen her that jealous and I found this both attractive and unpleasant.

"Strange women? Is there any other kind?" I asked lightly. Rose laughed but I could still see the green-eyed dragon. So I added, "Do you really think anyone on this earth could measure up to you in my eyes, sweetheart? Your presence in my life is the best argument I know for a benevolent God."

Rose opened her mouth to make a smart reply but her face fell apart and she began crying. It took me a long time to comfort her and by the time I had, I was dead beat. The last thing I heard before I fell off the planet was her saying softly, "I love you, husband. That's the sweetest thing anyone has ever said to me."

I growled something inarticulate and Rose laughed. Later she told me it sounded like "Assholes!"

Rose was less than an hour gone when I was on the phone and talking with every Subaru dealership in the yellow pages. I insisted on talking to the sales manager and told each one exactly what I equipment I wanted. I also explained that this was a bid situation with no negotiation. "I want to close the deal this afternoon, cash and no trade, so call me back with your best price by noon." I gave them the number of a burner cell I'd bought earlier in the week just for this purpose. I had learned the hard way not to give out the number of my private phone to sales people.

Several of these folk tried to negotiate by phone but I simply hung up and went on to the next. When I was done calling through the list, a couple of would-be negotiators called me back and tried to engage me in dickering again. I hung up.

One determined soul called me back a third time, begging for a chance to make a deal. He said he would beat the price of any other dealer in the Metroplex. He also told me it might be hard to find what I was looking for locally.

I reminded the man of what I wanted and did not want, and I told him he had three units that fit the bill in his company's inventory. He wanted to know how I knew this and started to argue with me when I told him. I waited patiently until he had run down. "Let me give you a tip," I told him. "Sales 101. It doesn't matter whether you are selling girdles or golf clubs. You can never win an argument with a customer. Particularly when you're lying."

He spluttered and I hung up. Then the fellow tried to call me back. I don't know if he thought he could change my mind or wanted to cuss me out or what. I simply blocked his number and fixed myself some lunch. At two o'clock the dealer with the best price picked me up at the apartment and by five I was the proud owner of a brand new Forester. It was white with less than fifty miles on the clock and it would be ready by noon the next day. The delay was because I had ordered a trailer hitch installed. The dealer promised to call if there was a delay and to deliver it to our apartment by closing time the following afternoon. He also loaned me a courtesy car.

That evening I ate a lonely supper at the apartment and wondered why I had tolerated that for so long. After cleaning up I dug out my laptop to see if there was anything I felt like editing. I have found writing to be a strong defense against loneliness but that day it didn't work. So I was delighted when Rose called and we spent an hour visiting. "I really missed you today," I told her. "It's just not the same when you're not around."

Rose agreed, then teased. "Well, at least you get a little

rest. I seem to have trouble keeping my hands off you."

"I noticed that," I replied. "It's a terrible death to be....
Never mind."

"Bored to death?" she laughed. "You know what I miss
most right now?"

"I'm afraid to guess."

"No, I'm being serious. I miss your arms around me and
feeling you right next to me with nothing in between. I wish
I was there now."

"It's not nice to torment an old fellow like that," I told her
gently. Then I was overcome with the feeling of what she had
become in my life. "God, I love you, Rose."

"And I love you, too, Ralph," she answered sweetly. There
was a moment's silence. Then she asked. "So what have you
been up to today?"

"Doing a little research and taking care of some business,"
I temporized. "Nothing to write home about."

"You're up to something, aren't you?" she asked.

"At the moment I'm not up to anything but talking with
you. How was your day?"

"Very strange. Things went well this afternoon when I
talked to my advisor. He thought it was a good thing getting
in-depth interviews with one of the people I'm writing
about. He told me I should do the same with the others, if
possible." She laughed.

It was my turn to ride the green eyed dragon. I tried to
fight it but something must have crept into my voice. "You're
jealous, aren't you?" she asked.

"I'm trying damned hard not to be," I told her. "I'm failing
miserably. I've never felt this way about anyone, Rose. Not
even Angela. You are the woman of my dreams."

"I'm sorry," she told me. "I didn't intend to make you
jealous. I really need you to trust me."

"I do, Rose, completely. I don't know where this is coming from but it's not your problem. It's mine and I will deal with it as best I can." Then I chuckled.

"What?" Rose asked sharply.

"It's my crazy writer's mind. I just wondered what it would be like showing up at Saint Patrick's for confession. I'm not going to do so, but it struck me as funny."

"That sounds like deflecting humor," she told me. "What's wrong with seeing if it would help? It doesn't have to be at the cathedral, either."

I thought about that. "You may be right but at the moment I'm more interested in you. Anything else happen?"

"As a matter of fact, there was. I hoped to be able to avoid Grace completely but she showed up as I was unloading the car. She wanted to know why I was driving a car with Minnesota plates. I told her I borrowed it from a friend but she wasn't satisfied with that. She wanted to know who my friend was and where I'd been all week."

She sighed and I knew something had really bothered her. As strong a soul as she is, I couldn't imagine what that might be. "I'm sorry you had to deal with that, Rose," I said. "Did something else happen?"

"No, not really, and Grace is not what's bothering me. I'm afraid I lost it, Ralph. One moment I thought I was perfectly calm and the next I was a raving bitch. It wasn't what I said, either. It was how I said it that bothered me."

"What did you say?"

"I told her it wasn't any of her bleepity bleep-bleep concern and to mind her own efffity-eff-eff business. And to keep her big effity-bleep-bleep snout out of mine." Then she snickered. "That came out of nowhere and it scared her so bad she peed her panties."

Rose laughed but then she became serious again. "The

thing is, Ralph, it scared me, too. What really bothers me is how out of control I was. I'm glad I didn't have a big stick in my hand. It took me half an hour to stop shaking."

"It sounds like she may have had it coming," I replied. "From everything you've told me, she can't be easy to live with. Do you think she would have even heard you if you hadn't been that... forceful?"

"No, and that's what I keep telling myself. Not that it helps. I hate it, but I need to apologize."

"For how you said it, maybe. Maybe for letting it build up so long, too, but not for telling her the truth. Was your other roommate there when it happened? Gail?"

"Yes, Gail was helping me unload," Rose replied.

"What was her take on the situation?"

"She said it was pretty emphatic. That's the word she used. She thought I was going to slug Grace. She also said it was a long time overdue."

"Does Gail know about us?"

"She does now. I picked up take-out on the way home this evening and told her while we ate."

This surprised me. "Was Grace there when you did?"

"No, she was hiding out in her room. Gail and I ate on the deck and Grace may have been eavesdropping. She does that. Anyway, Grace and I are not speaking, apparently, which is fine by me. I'd like it best if I never had to see her again."

"So what are your plans?" I asked.

"I thought I might pack up my stuff tonight. Almost everything will fit in the Forester except for a few things like my bike. I'm thinking about giving it to Gail to use. Cowtown doesn't seem very bike friendly to me."

"You might be surprised. On the other hand, we could always mount one of those big-assed brush bumpers on the front."

Rose chuckled. "They only weigh, what? Ten times as much as my bike?"

"More like twenty times," I assured her. "I tried to lift one in the dealership."

"Tried? You mean you couldn't?"

"The problem is I'm not thirty any more. I could have handled it easily then."

"You know what? I'm glad you're not thirty, Ralph. I like you just the way you are."

"I'll remind you of that the next time you're pissed at me."

"That might not be the wisest approach,"she warned me. She said this lightly but I sensed an iron resolve behind her words.

"Then I'd probably better not do it. So are you planning to be home tomorrow night?"

"I think so but I may wait and get a fresh start the day after. I've got a couple of errands to run and the traffic coming down here was awful."

"Well, be safe. That's the main thing." I started to tell her I loved her again but stopped myself, unsure how it might be taken.

I felt blue after I had hung up. I didn't feel like reading anything I saw around the apartment so I went online. The fare was even worse so I decided to go for a walk. There was a well tended park with a playscape several blocks from our place and I contented myself watching the antics of the kids on the equipment. I had been there for maybe a half hour or so before one of the women in a group walked over and sat down on the other end of the bench. "How you doing?" she asked after a while.

"I'm doing fine," I assured her. I wasn't in the mood for company and while I wasn't being surly, I wasn't exactly friendly, either.

We must have sat there five minutes before she spoke to me again. "Come here often?" she asked, a bit too casually.

I turned and looked at her directly. She didn't appear to be a hooker but who knows these days? "Look," I said. "I don't know what you want but I'm not in the market. I'm in a committed relationship and right now I simply want to be alone." The woman glared at me and I shrugged and turned back toward the playscape.

"I want to see some identification," I heard her say. When I turned around she was standing up and holding up a badge.

"Where's your probable cause, officer?" I asked calmly, remaining still.

"Are you refusing to identify yourself?" she demanded.

"Not at all," I answered, not moving and keeping my voice civil. "I'm sitting here quietly going about my lawful private business. I am asking why you need to see my identification."

"Show me some ID!" she demanded, raising her voice. Some of the people near the playscape turned and looked at us.

"Very well. It's in my left hip pocket and my billfold is black." I carefully extracted my driver's license and laid it on the bench between us. I was careful to make no sudden moves.

The officer carefully looked at my driver's license and then called it into the dispatcher. "This says you're from Minnesota. What are you doing here in Fort Worth?"

"Among other things, I'm thawing out," I told her. When I said this one of the people near the kids laughed. This did nothing to improve things with the police officer. "I'm also undergoing medical treatment," I added.

"What for?"

"With all due respect, officer, that is privileged information. I will tell you I got sick on the way home from Austin and had to stay over down here."

Just then the officer's radio crackled to life, telling everyone in earshot there were no wants or warrants in the system for me. She looked at my license again and reluctantly handed it back. "I'll be keeping an eye on you," she said in a loud voice and turned to walk off.

"Just a moment, officer," called out in an equally loud voice. "I need your badge number and the name of your supervisor." The officer turned her head and glared at me but didn't stop. "Are you refusing to identify yourself, officer?" I called out but she kept going.

I walked over to the people near the playscape and asked what the name of the park might be. One of the mothers answered me and I thanked her and wrote it down in my notepad. I also noted the time and date of the incident.

"Are you a lawyer?" one of the other women asked.

"Not guilty," I told her.

"Well, you look familiar. I can't figure out where I saw you."

"It could have been on the dust jacket of one of my books," I suggested.

"Oh, that's it. Now I remember. You must be James Patterson," she said.

"No, I'm not that rich," I replied, smiling, and the group laughed. I dug out a business card and handed it to her.

"Oh!" she declared. "You're Cody Adams. You wrote that naughty book."

"I think of it more as a love story," I told her. "I didn't set out to be naughty. I thought it was pretty tame by today's standards."

"Are you going to file a complaint?" one of the other women asked.

"Probably not," I said. "I am going to talk with her

supervisor. She was way off base."

"She was just looking out for our kids," the second woman insisted.

"I understand that and that's why I probably will not file a formal complaint. It's the brass who are at fault here. She should have been better trained."

"What are you doing here, anyway?" the woman insisted.

"I was enjoying watching the kids play. They have a lot to teach us about ourselves if we watch and listen. We only live a couple of blocks up the street."

"So you're married?" one of the women asked.

"I'm trying to get that way," I said and they laughed.

Rose thought it was funny when I told her about the conversation late that evening when she called again. "I just needed to hear your voice," she told me. "That's why I called. I seem to be getting very attached to a sweet man named Ralph and I really miss him."

"Well, Ralph misses his Texas Rose. How in the world did I ever live without you?"

"Well, for the first three decades I hadn't been born. So you were out of luck. Then you were busy being married to Angela and writing all those books and getting famous. So you didn't even know I was around. You want me to go on?"

"You know, I could listen to you read the phone book," I told her. "Just the sound of your voice does something very special to me."

"Are you sure that's not simply the memory of my, um, accouterments? That seems to do something to you."

"Accouterments or hooterments?"

"You're bad, but at least you noticed."

"How could I not?"

I was pleasantly surprised when Rose arrived at just after

four the next afternoon. "Neither of the people I needed to see were in town and I didn't want to hang around," she told me, holding me close. "I was packed and I didn't want another scene with Grace, either. So I came ahead."

"I'm glad," I told her, kissing her with my full attention. She responded in kind and we suddenly found ourselves entwined on the floor, tossing aside our clothing and making love like there was no tomorrow.

"Mmm," Rose murmured as we lay resting in one another's arms a while later, still joined. "Somebody really missed me."

"Since before you were born," I replied lightly.

Even so, Rose's eyes filled with tears and she held me tight against her. "You say the sweetest things, Ralph."

"I mean them, too," I assured her.

Any response Rose might have made was interrupted by a loud knock. "Mister Williams?" a loud voice sounded. "This is Sammy. I'm here from Harrison-Page. We need to swap keys."

Rose looked at me, frowning. "A little surprise," I told her. Turning toward the door I called out. "Be right there, Sammy."

We grabbed our clothes and ran to the bedroom. I pulled on some trousers and the tee-shirt I had been wearing and slipped into some loafers. Checking myself in the bathroom mirror I combed my hair with my fingers and headed for the door. Through the peep-hole I saw one of the young men I knew from the dealership.

"What was that all about?" Rose asked after I shut the door. She was in the jeans and top she had worn home and it was evident she was not pleased.

"It was about me having some fun," I replied. "Put on some shoes and I'll show you."

When we walked out of the building, Rose spotted the

new Forester right away. "I always wanted a white one," I told her as we walked over to the new ride. "They don't come in yellow but it's much safer."

Rose wasn't buying, not for a moment. She glared at me, then burst into tears and rushed back into our apartment. I followed immediately but by the time I got inside our bedroom door was shut. When I turned the doorknob lightly, I discovered it was locked.

Not knowing what else to do, I went out to the older Forester and unloaded the suitcase and overnight kit I had carried out when Rose left the day she headed for Austin. I decided the rest could wait. The bedroom door was still shut when I took in the luggage and I started to go for a walk. Then it occurred to me that Rose might not be there when I got back and that frightened me. I really didn't think that would happen but I wasn't willing to take the chance. I would never have expected her to react the way she just had, either. It was at that moment I realized I really didn't know this woman very well and I was overwhelmed by a numbing fear. It felt like my world was falling apart again, just like it had when Angela died.

There was no question in my mind I could survive the loss of Rose. One of the things I had learned after Angela's death was that I could survive such a loss, step by step, one day at a time. The question was whether I would want to. Having found the woman of my dreams after a lifetime of searching, I had somehow ruined the very thing that had brought me back to life again. I had done so with the best of intentions, and had no idea quite how it happened. Or why. Nor in my wildest dreams could I ever expect to find this kind of love again.

All these thoughts collided in my mind like a twenty-car freeway pileup. Somehow I found my way outside to the picnic table where Rose and I often sat to watch the day come to life. I don't know how long I sat there looking into an abyss of empty days and years that I thought lay before me. I lost all track of time, not caring nor really noticing the afternoon light dim into gloaming. At some point I became aware that my feet were hurting but somehow that didn't seem to matter. After a while the pain went away, fading into nothing. A detached part of myself wondered if I was dying, but at that moment it didn't matter. Dying seemed like a mercy, a severe one, perhaps, but still a gift.

I suppose I might have sat there all night as I apparently had at Saint Patrick's. Nor could I tell you much about the city life going on around me. I seem to have stopped looking into the abyss at some point and had entered it. Nor was this unpleasant, for there was nothing there, nothing to worry about. This is a trick I learned as a child when things were very bad, and it got me through the awful time after Angela died. For there was no pain in the emptiness, no grief or sorrow. Yet there was no joy, either, and a detached part of myself felt sad about this. Yet the feeling was isolated in the complete silence of the Void and was somehow not attached to me. The greater part of me simply felt relief in the vast emptiness. Nothing more would be required of me, and while I was there, I would not make a shambles of anything else.

I talked about this to a counselor about this once. I was surprised at what she had to say. She told me the symptoms I had were common to traumatized children. Like prisoners or soldiers, children are trapped in a situation they cannot control but upon which they must depend for everything they need. They protect themselves by dissociation, which is what I had done with the Void.

Once they are out of the abusive situation children may

be able to construct an almost normal life but they also show the same symptoms as adult victims of combat trauma. Like shell shocked vets they cannot handle the prolonged stress of normal living very well. So when normal life dumps its nasty surprises on them, they develop very distinct symptoms.

Among these symptoms are withdrawal from the things that once gave them pleasure. Another is a self imposed isolation. Survivors build emotional walls to protect themselves from further injury, but in shutting out the bad stuff, these walls also prevent life-giving things like joy and delight from entering. They build habits of self protection that reinforce their withdrawal from life and many of these poor souls become insane. They resort to drugs or alcohol or risk taking, and many of them often suicide to end their torment.

Then there are those who become like a cancer in the society that gave them life. They become predators who express their pain by taking the lives of those who have done them no wrong. The best example I know is the childhood story of Hannibal Lecter.

It was as a tortured child that I created the safe haven I later came to call the Void, and much later, the Abyss. It was there I took my rage to be soothed and quieted, and it was there this rage unintentionally spawned my personal demons. These in turn became monsters for the lack of life and love and simple delight. These healing things were shut out by the ramparts I built to protect myself from hurt.

It was only much later, with the help of a wise physician of souls, that I began to allow these things into my life and to allow healing to take place. I am painfully aware it could have gone either way. I have no idea why I was spared the awful doom of becoming a raging cancer in the belly of the beast we call civilization. Yet I was spared, to whatever end, and for that I am very grateful.

That evening I sat there in silence, not thinking or allowing myself to feel the fear and sadness that was crushing my soul. Then at some point I felt someone touch my face and a gentle voice called to me from outside the Void. I was surprised by this and at first I was angry about the intrusion. Then the darkness cleared for a moment and I saw the outline of someone standing in front of me.

At first I thought it was Angela and I was filled with overwhelming joy. Then I remembered she was many years dead and the memory was like a lance. Even so, a flicker of hope touched the emptiness inside me when I thought it might be Rose. Then I remembered that Rose was gone, too, and knowing this was devastating. I began to weep bitterly.

It was then that someone cradled my head in her arms and held me gently in my grief. "Ralph?" a soft voice spoke. It sounded like Rose and the arms embracing me felt like her and I wondered how this could be. Then the darkness lifted once again. I realized that it really was Rose and the floodgates burst within me. I clung to her like a drowning man to a life ring.

After a while Rose pulled back a bit and spoke again. "Ralph? We need to go inside. It's not safe out here." I nodded but when I tried to move my feet it felt like a thousand needles shooting up and down my legs, embedding themselves and then tearing free. Even so, I kept moving, almost grateful for the pain, and somehow we made it into the building. Thank God there was an elevator. I don't know how I would have ever managed the stairs.

By the time we reached our apartment, my legs and feet felt something like normal. Rose wanted me to lie down but I told her I needed to keep moving for a while. "The more I move my legs the more my mind clears," I explained. "I probably should have gone for a walk."

"Why didn't you?" she asked.

"I was afraid that you might leave before I got back and that I'd never see you again," I told her. "So I sat down and tried to figure what I had done to make you so angry. Then I guess I blacked out."

"It wasn't you that made me angry," she told me. "It was something awful that happened to me a long time ago. Quite often. I'll try to explain it tomorrow." She looked at me gravely. "You know, there's one thing you need to get through your thick Viking skull, Ralph. I'm here for as long as we last. And I do mean 'we,' you and me, and not 'it.' So get used to it, mister."

"You mean 'til death do us part?" I asked, not quite believing what I was hearing.

"Yes, but I want to wait a while before we make it official." Seeing the look in my eye, she smiled. "Yes, I know. At this season of life time is of the essence, but we'll have time. I promise."

Rose paused and then grinned. It was like the sun coming out after a hard winter. I felt my spirits begin to lift. "It's like a fungus, Ralph. We need to give it a little time to let the idea grow on us."

I laughed, but it sounded hollow in my ears. "How romantic! May I quote you?"

"It's not original," Rose told me. She got up and began to unbutton my shirt. "Let's get some rest now and just hold each other for a while. Tomorrow we'll look at Ralph's new toy."

5

A Sacred Thing Called Play

I still felt rocky the next morning and my aching legs got me up early. They reminded me of their mistreatment and it took me a while to work out the kinks. Yet it was a bright spring morning and I suggested we pay a visit to the Japanese gardens. Despite our apartment being so close by we had somehow never gotten around to visiting either the gardens or the zoo.

"The zoo will probably be jam packed today," I pointed out as we were talking about this. "I expect Saturdays and Sundays always are. The Zen gardens probably won't be if we get there fairly soon. Or we could do something else."

"I'd vote for something else," Rose said, stacking our breakfast dishes in the sink. She walked around the kitchen table and sat in my lap, giving me a kiss that left no doubt what she had in mind. "We need to talk and hold each other. Maybe we can go for a walk in the park later and take a picnic. I want to see your new machine, too."

"For sure?" I asked and she nodded. "We don't have to keep it if you don't like it," I added.

"Are you kidding?" she asked, grinning. "I took a peek out the window when I made coffee. It looks wonderful." Then she shook her head. "I really don't know what happened to me last night, Ralph. I think everything caught up with me all at once."

I must have looked puzzled so she began to count on her fingers. "Think about it, about all we have on our plates right now. First we met each other and ran off to Cowtown for a wonderful week. Then you got sick, which meant we had to set up housekeeping here. You had to quit teaching, at least for a while, and I had to rearrange my life. Now we're in love and talking about marriage, and all of this has happened within the last month. I think moving from Austin and the thing with Grace threw me on overload. I'm sorry I took it out on you last night. Most of what's happened is wonderful and I wouldn't change a thing. Yet even the good changes have been stressful. We haven't had time to live into them."

"So it wasn't about me being sneaky and buying the new Forester."

"No, not directly. The thing is, the first guy I fell for used to manipulate me with stuff like that. I told you about him, the first guy I almost married."

I nodded. "And now here's this strange old man who blew in with the north wind who's doing what looks like the same thing. The difference is that this old man really means it, Rose. I really did want to surprise you."

"I know," Rose replied. "It just took me a little while to remember that. I'm so sorry, Ralph."

"No, Rose, you're wonderful. I don't know why I took it so personally. What I'm having trouble with right now is believing it's real. I keep expecting to wake up and find out this was only a wonderful dream."

"That's why we need to give ourselves some time to live into it," Rose said, smiling. "Time for the fungus to grow. You're not alone, you know. I'm afraid of the same things."

"So how do we do that?" I said, trying not to grin like a monkey. "How do we learn to live with the fear?"

"Well, I have an idea where we could start," she said giving me a wicked look.

"I hoped you might."

We had a wonderful afternoon that day, walking around

our new neighborhood. We packed a lunch and ate it at the park with the playscape. Some of the same mothers were there as had been the afternoon I was accosted by the new sergeant. A couple of them waved and came over to where we were sitting. One of them pulled out a copy of *Midlife Crazy* and asked if I would mind autographing it. "Of course not," I told her. "How do you want me to make it out?"

"So is this the lady you're trying to marry?" the other woman asked. She looked pointedly at Rose's left hand.

"We haven't gotten around to a ring yet," Rose volunteered smoothly, smiling. "We're thinking about Christmas, if not sooner, but there's no rush."

"You can thank your lucky stars for that," the third woman said. She had followed the other two and joined us. "We had an awful time trying to go to school and raise a baby. We're still together, though. A lot of our friends who waited aren't."

"So you decided to file a complaint with the police supervisor." The second lady said. It was a statement, a challenge and not a question.

"No, actually, I didn't. I'm not sure it would do much good."

"You didn't?" the third lady asked, surprised. "Her supervisor came and talked to us yesterday evening."

"Good," I said. "Then I don't need to bother him. He's aware of the situation and he's doing something about it."

"He told us your real name isn't Cody Adams," the first lady said. There was a strong hint of accusation in her voice.

"It's not," I assured her. "Cody Grey Adams is my registered trademark. I use it when I write love stories. I have other pen names I use for writing westerns and other genres."

"Why do you do that?"

"For the same reason Samuel Clemens wrote as Mark Twain, to protect my privacy. I have a day job career, too. Or

I did. It looks like I'll be retiring from that. Then I'm going to tour the world with my beautiful bride." I dropped my voice to a conspiratorial whisper. "You'd never know it to look at her but she's older than I am."

"Mister Adams has been known to stretch the truth," Rose pointed out dryly. She glanced at her watch and then at me. "We better get going if we're going to be there when Sally comes."

"Sally?" I asked when we were out of earshot.

"Oh, you know, Silly Sally Simple Simon's sister."

"Oh, I thought you meant Sally the limerick girl."

Rose sighed. "All right, I'll bite. Let's hear it."

I thought for a moment and then began to recite.

> There once was a maiden named Sally
> Who occasionally liked to dally.
> She sat on the lap
> Of a well endowed chap
> And said "Peter, you're right up my alley."

"That's awful!" Rose snorted with a grin.

"Yeah, but you liked it. There's something about limericks that seems to grab people. I think it's because they're naughty but not mean spirited. They poke fun at us all."

"Naughty? I'd say downright bawdy. Do you know any that aren't?"

"Sure, a lot of the older ones aren't. Edward Lear published a whole book of clean limericks for children. I think it was about 1850 and he called it *A Book of Nonsense*. But there were clean ones around before that. There's the one about the cats of Kilkenny. It's an Irish nursery rhyme."

"Recite it for me," she challenged and I did.

> There once were two cats in Kilkenny.
> For each it was one cat to many.

So they hissed and they spit
And they clawed and they bit,
'Til instead of two cats there weren't any.

"Now that's good," Rose said. "I wonder how limericks got so bawdy?"

"Are you kidding? A lot of them came out of pubs, especially Irish pubs. Customers would stand around and try to outdo each other. They still do. It's a form of folk art."

Rose laughed. "Not according to one of my professors. She says it's doggerel, not real poetry."

"Doggerel? I used to know what that means. Isn't it just a polite way of saying 'bitch?'"

"You're awful," Rose assured me.

"No, I'm a writer. They pay me to bend words. Seriously, though. Language is a living thing, like a race horse. It's meant to be run through the course, not just pull a plow."

As we walked around the neighborhood we fell into a companionable silence. When we got back to our apartment I was surprised when Rose suggested we sit at the picnic table instead of going inside. "There's something I need to talk about," she told me.

Once we sat down, she came right to the point. "Unless I counted wrong, I'm about two weeks late this time," she said. Her eyes searched my face. "And I'm never late."

"Wonderful!" I declared. "At least I think so. How do you feel about it?"

"I think it's wonderful, too, Ralph, but it scares me. I'm thirty-eight now and with older mothers there's a greater chance of the child having birth defects. With an older father there's a high risk, too. I'm not sure I could deal with that."

"All right, but can't they test for that? Something about testing the amniotic fluid in the womb?"

Rose nodded. "Yes, amniocentesis, AFT. The problem

with that is that even doing the test can cause miscarriage. What bothers me is having to make the decision to abort if the test comes back positive. The only good outcome of the test is a negative result."

"I think the final decision is yours, Rose. I will support whatever that may be. For better or for worse, as the vows say."

"What if we get a positive result for birth defects? How would you feel then?"

"I have no idea what I'll feel until we get there," I replied. "Regardless of how I may feel, I would encourage you to go ahead with the abortion if you test positive. I will not be the one who has to carry the burden down the years. So it has to be your choice."

Rose nodded and began to cry. I took her in my arms and held her until she pulled back. "That's what I thought you'd say but I had to be sure," she told me. "Why don't you take me for a drive in your new Forester?"

"Our new Forester," I corrected and she smiled. "Are you sure you want the old fart to drive?"

"Yes, until you get the first dent or scratch."

We went to see the doctor a few days later and she was not surprised when we told her Rose might be pregnant. "I wondered when you first came in," she smiled. "A lot of my practice is in gynecology and pregnant women tend to have a certain luminosity, for lack of a better term. They look radiant and their skin is really beautiful. A big part of my job is convincing them of that. Am I to assume Ralph is the father?"

Rose laughed. "It was either him or the Holy Ghost," she declared, then quickly apologized. "I'm sorry. I don't know where that came from. I hope I didn't offend you."

Doctor Anne smiled. "Actually, that was a new one on me.

It was amusing. With all due reverence," she added. "I do need to ask if there are any religious issues if terminating the pregnancy is indicated."

Rose looked and me and we both shook our heads. The good doctor nodded. "Very well, the AFT procedure needs to be done from fourteen to sixteen weeks from conception. When do you think that was?"

I sat back and listened while the two women worked out the details using a paper calendar. When they were done, the doctor looked at me. "You seem pleased with this news, Ralph. Are there any issues you need to discuss?"

I shook my head. "No, I helped raise two children and both of them turned out well. It was challenging at the time but wonderful, too. I'm looking forward to doing it again."

"Remember that when it's your turn to do diapers," Rose declared.

"It's definitely going to be disposables," I replied. "Diaper pails are over the top."

Doctor Anne grimaced and nodded. "You're right. They stink and they're horribly unsanitary."

"So what do you think?" Rose asked once we were in the car. So far it had not acquired its first dent or scratch and I was still driving.

"I think we're in for a great adventure," I replied. "I hope we have more than one child but that's entirely up to you. Your health is the prime consideration."

"Speaking of prime, your wife to be needs to be fed, Mister Williams. I crave red meat!"

"My wife to be? Does that mean it's time to pick out a ring, Missus Williams? Or do you prefer to be Mistress?"

"Mistress is actually more correct."

"You didn't exactly answer my question, my love."

"Let's go with mistress. It sounds racier."

"Not to push, but you know very well I was referring to my first question, picking a ring."

Rose looked scared. "I can't think of a good reason for putting it off."

I nodded. "I gather you would prefer to let things fungus a little more."

Rose laughed. "I knew I was going to regret that the moment I said it."

I shrugged. "Well, do you mind my talking around or about the subject?" She shook her head.

"Well, there are some basic questions I need to know. Do you prefer to be involved in picking a ring out or do you trust my judgment?"

"Since it's a gift, I think I need to trust your judgment. What did you have in mind?"

"Oh, that's easy. I was thinking of this god-awful heap of diamonds and rubies and emeralds."

Rose looked aghast. "Tell me you're kidding me, Ralph. Please."

"Of course, I am. Tacky is not for my bride. I was actually thinking of a solitaire, a natural emerald rather than a diamond. I prefer yellow gold to white but either will do. What's important is how it's set. I think a bezel setting that protects the stone is better than a raised stone like most engagement and wedding rings. I was thinking more in terms of an ancient look rather than a modern traditional. I think it needs to reflect how I see you and our marriage."

I was parking the car at the restaurant when I said the last sentence. When I looked at Rose I saw tears in her eyes. I reached out to hold her but she stopped me with a hand. "Let me get this out before I fall apart. "The answer is 'yes,' Ralph."

"All right," I said gently. "Just to be clear, yes to...?"

"Yes, I will marry you and yes it can be as soon as you want. Yes, you can pick out the ring, and yes, we can live here in Texas or move me to Minnesota with you."

"Wow!" I declared. My hand shook as I took the keys out of the ignition. "I wasn't expecting all that, Rose. I don't know what to say. Or do I need to leap on the top of the car and dance around and howl?"

Rose laughed. "You need to kiss your fiancé, silly man."

I did so, thoroughly. "Now you need to feed me," Rose declared. "Prime rib. I'm eating for two."

"Or maybe for three," I said.

"Now wouldn't that be a hoot?"

We had a lot of fun together getting ready for the baby. One of the first questions was where we wanted to live. This was driven by where we wanted to raise our family, and like many people our top priority was schools. The quickest way of getting information was the Internet and we were careful what sites we chose to use. What surprised me was the results we got. Among the very top ranked states was Wyoming, and to me it was obvious why. Where people spend their money gives a pretty clear picture of priorities, and Wyoming was the top state in school finance. When it came to overall grading and achievement, it came in, in seventh place.

When we looked at the scores for Texas, we discovered that the lone star state was in the middle on every scale we looked at. Out of curiosity I looked at Minnesota and discovered the north star state came in eleventh over all. The only other states that caught my attention were New Hampshire and Washington.

"So what do you think?" I asked my wife to be.

"Texas is out as far as I'm concerned," she told me without hesitation. "People seem to be mean-spirited down here.

Rednecks, white socks, and piss poor beer. They like killing people, too. To hell with compassion. Slip the bastards the needle and let God sort it out."

She paused. "I'm ranting, aren't I?" I shrugged and she smiled. "Wyoming, on the other hand, might be interesting. I love the mountains."

I nodded. "It's a wonderful place for adults," I told her. "I'm not sure I'd like to raise a child there. It's one of the most intolerant, racist places I've ever lived. I'm not sure why, either. In some ways it's almost radical. It was the first state that allowed women to vote."

"When did you live there?" Rose asked.

"Several years ago I spent a semester lecturing at the university in Laramie. I was amazed at what I heard people there telling me. It's not a state to be a person of color."

"What about Minnesota?" Rose asked. "You have friends there."

"I also have a comfortable house on the lake. Winters can get pretty bitter but that's why I drive a Forester. There's lots to do there, too, and attitudes tend to be far more liberal. The question is how you would like it."

"The only problem I can see is that your house is Angela's home. What happens when I want to change things?"

"Except for my study and workshop, I'd like to think that would be fine. It's probably time for a general remodeling."

"You'd like to think. So you're not sure you want someone messing with Angela's home."

"Actually, it's mostly knowing where things are. One of Angela's faults was getting bored just as I was getting used to the latest arrangement and changing everything around. Except for my study and workshop, but the workshop's a separate building."

"You know what? I think we need to spend this summer

in Minnesota. I may love the place exactly the way it is. What are you smiling about?"

"Oh, I was thinking about the looks on some of my friends' faces when I show up with a beautiful young bride. And a child on the way."

"You could always pass me off as your live-in nurse, grandpa. Then they could be scandalized when my tummy grows. Or are they the kind of people to be scandalized?"

"Some of them, yes. Most if them, no, unless it's something like plagiarism. I think I would prefer to get quietly married before we head north. I know you want a proper wedding and we can have one once we're settled. Maybe this winter. You don't need to be worrying about a wedding until your thesis is done. That's very important to me, your finishing your degree."

"This winter I'll look like I swallowed the whole pumpkin," Rose pointed out. Then she looked at me thoughtfully. "Why is my degree so important to you?"

"One reason is that academics can be such snobs when it comes to degrees. Having your master's makes you a member of the club. It helps break the ice."

"So does being scandalous, but you said one reason. Are there others?"

"Well, yes. With the degree you can get a job teaching after I'm gone if there's need."

"Ralph, if I need a job I can always go back to nursing," she said, surprising me. "I guess I didn't tell you about that, did I? My undergraduate degree was a BSN and I kept up my license when I went back to school. I pick up shifts whenever I need extra money. Beats hooking." She added, laughing.

"You never cease to amaze me, Rose," I told her. "I had no idea I was getting together with a nurse. I guess that really does make you my live-in nurse. Why the change?"

"I kind of burned out on nursing. I worked intensive care for a long time and there was a high turnover rate there. Then I shifted to trauma and spent too many nights in the ER. I worked a lot of double shifts there, too. It was better than going home to an empty house after Gabe died. But I didn't want to give up my license when I quit. I worked too hard for it."

"Gabe as in Gabriel?" I asked and she nodded, smiling. "So we were both matched up with angels," I pointed out.

Rose nodded and grinned. "So mind your p's and q's, Buster. You've got a hard act to follow. We both do."

"Maybe we both need to lay them to rest," I said, speaking mostly to myself. Then I realized something. "That's why you want to wait, isn't it? It feels like marrying me would be like betraying Gabe." Rose nodded but she wouldn't meet my eyes. "I apologize, Rose," I told her. "I had no idea what was happening." I reached out and touched her face. "We don't have to do a thing until you're ready," I added.

Rose looked up and she was smiling. "Well, there is a child on the way, Mister. You knocked me up in case you haven't heard."

"I recall having some help, Missus. I think we were both knocking pretty hard."

"Maybe you better remind me, husband."

Later, when we were lying quietly holding each other in our arms, she said, "It's time, Ralph. It's time."

We were married a week later by a county judge with two of his office people to witness. Since the wedding was at nine in the morning we celebrated with brunch at Pappadeux and paid a visit to the Fort Worth zoo. It was the only opportunity we would have. We were scheduled to leave for Minnesota in a couple of days and somehow had never taken time to visit the critters.

Since it was a weekday there were very few visitors there and we had a delightful time watching the staff care for the animals. Rose was quite taken with the flamingos and the white tigers and asked to borrow my camera. She had given me a hard time for bringing along a camera bag and her eyes grew wide when she saw what I pulled out of the case. It was a new Canon Rebel. I thought about getting her the 7D but the t2i weights more than two pounds less and I got that. I also ordered a Tamron 28-300 zoom lens to go with it. This was the same combination I had used for years and the only difference between hers and mine was the bright rainbow neck strap I put on hers.

"I thought you forgot your main camera at home," she said. "Why haven't you been using it?"

"This isn't my camera," I told her. "I bought this as a wedding present for my bride. That's why I didn't give it to you until now. The case goes with it."

Rose took the camera gingerly. "I don't know how to use it," she said.

I nodded. "I went ahead and set it up on automatic mode. The manual is in the case but you don't need it right now. All you need to do is point and shoot. It's got a 16 meg SD card in it and another one in the case. There's also a spare battery, fully charged."

Rose's eyes filled with tears. "Oh, Ralph, thank you. You didn't have to do this." She hugged my neck.

"I know, my love, but I wanted to. I had fun at the waterpark watching you hop around trying to catch the little people in action. You seemed to be having a lot of fun with it, too."

"You're spending way too much on me," she said. "First the new Forester, and then furnishing the apartment and buying the ring. Are you sure you can afford it?"

I laughed. "The books have done very well," I told her. "Money is the least of my worries. The house is paid for and I haven't had anyone or anything to spend money on for the last eight years." I shrugged. "So I've banked my whole paycheck. Why not spend it on us while we can enjoy it?"

Rose looked at me a long time and then grinned. "So how does this work?" she said, turning on the power and pointing the camera directly at me. I heard the shutter snap three times in quick succession." Talk about candid camera," she laughed, showing me the display.

I looked like a drooling idiot in all three shots. I had opened my mouth to say something in the first and blinked in the third, and the camera had caught me at my worst. The last shot caught me with my mouth shut and I looked like I was drunk. "Let's try it again," Rose said sweetly, moving to one side. "Just you and the rhino."

This time I was ready and again Rose caught a burst of three. "I need to change that over to single shots," she said frowning. Then she looked at the display and laughed. "Wow, I don't know if I want anyone else to see this or not." When she showed me the display I saw what she meant. I was grinning in all three and there was a glint in my eye that was unmistakable. "That makes me hot just looking at it," Rose said, slipping into my arms and giving me a kiss that left me weak in the knees.

"Maybe we need to frame it and put it by our beside," I suggested.

We took our time taking in the rest of the zoo that afternoon and spent the evening eating pizza and making love. The day seemed to slip away so quickly I felt a little sad when we said goodnight. Yet when I got up in the night, Rose was awake when I got back to bed and we held each other skin to skin until it was light outside. Then we began our first married morning together by making gentle love once more.

We finished shutting down the apartment that morning and getting ready to move to Minnesota. There really wasn't that much left to do. Rose had never gotten around to unpacking most of her stuff from Austin so it went back into the older Forester. The Good Will people were glad to send a truck for our furniture and kitchen stuff, and what little stuff I'd acquired went into our new car. Then we spent our last night in Cowtown in a motel and headed north early the next morning. Since we were driving against the incoming flow of traffic we made good time and spent the night in Emporia, Kansas.

The next morning we got an early start and easily made it to Sioux Falls by late afternoon. There is an IHOP there and after pigging out on pancakes we stretched our legs walking around the Empire Mall. Leaving there we spotted a Half Price Books store and spent a pleasant hour perusing their stock. I was surprised when Rose pointed out a couple of my books on the shelves. She gave me a saucy grin and murmured, "I even slept with the author."

Even though Rose said this softly, a passing patron overheard her and gave us a startled look. She was even more startled when Rose showed her my picture on the back cover. As we were checking out a while later we saw her talking to the clerk and nodding toward us. Rose thought this was funny.

The next morning I told Rose I had a surprise for her. She wanted to know what it was but I told her that would ruin the surprise. Nor was she any less confused when I told her to bring her camera.

So we left the car she was driving and I followed the

directions from a pamphlet I'd spotted in the motel lobby. Fortunately, Sioux Falls is a town that's fairly easy to navigate. I was able to find our way to the Butterfly House without getting lost.

Rose was delighted. "Someone told me about this a long time ago and I always wanted to see it," I explained. "I thought you might like it, too."

"I love butterflies!" she said. "I didn't know they did things like this."

As it turned out, the place had an aquarium, too, and it was past noon before we knew it. "That was fun," Rose told me over a late lunch at an Italian place not far from the mall. "Thank you. What else do you have up your sleeve." Seeing the look on my face she laughed and said, "I'm getting to know you, big guy. I know when you're up to something."

"Well, there's something else I haven't seen in a long time," I told her. "It's called the Corn Palace and it's about sixty miles west of here. It's truly unique."

"That sounds like a comedy show," she chuckled. "It might be fun. I like doing stuff with you. We don't have to be anywhere else do we?"

We ended up staying another night at the motel and drove to Mitchell together in the new Forester. We still hadn't collected a scratch or a dent but Rose liked the high speed limit on the freeway and agreed to drive. "Not to complain," she said to me, "but you drive like my grandmother."

"Is she still alive?" I asked.

"No she's been gone a long time. It was old age. She was ninety-three."

"That's precisely my point, assuming her death was not from wrecking her car."

We had a wonderful time at the Corn Palace. Rose was like a little kid, the way I hoped our child would be. While

Angela and I made a lot of the common mistakes people do when raising their children, it was a wonderful experience. Our kids had turned out well and their loss was a bitter experience. Even so, I was looking forward to doing it again and I was grateful for the opportunity. Then I realized that at my age it would be more like raising a grandchild.

The thing about visiting the Corn Place again was that the decor is completely redone every year or two. So it always looks different. Some years are better than others I am told, but the way it is put together is incredible. Nor can there be any doubt it is always somewhat corny, sometimes intentionally so.

Unfortunately, there was street repair going on and the outside view was obstructed by machinery. This did not stop Rose from going wild with her new camera, inside and out. Every evening on the road she had been devouring the user's manual and she had abandoned the automatic settings very quickly.

"That's a big part of the fun," she told me. "Getting to know your equipment so what you do is automatic. The light won't wait, so I can't be fumbling around figuring out what to do."

Rose was also one of those people who know how to make lemonade when life hands out lemons. When she was shooting the side of the Corn Palace where repairs were being done I noticed she spent a lot of time with the building equipment. I wondered why until I saw some of the images she had captured. I have no idea how she did this, but she produced the same effect she had with the cypress people at the water park. No longer was it inert mechanical equipment. It looked like living things, as if they were alive and about to do something. Nor could she tell me how she had done it.

"I don't know," she laughed when I asked. "I just see something and take a shot and I get lucky. I have no idea what I am doing until I see what I've done. It's more intuitive than planned. I guess I have a good eye."

"There's no guessing about it," I told her. "You have an incredible eye." Nor did I have any idea how unique her eye for an image was until she showed me some shots she had taken of me. Somehow it gave me an inkling of why she loved me so. It was as if I was looking at another man, one who I had never seen before but somehow had known by word of mouth for years.

The next morning we got an early start. This time I poured coal to the beast. Five hours after we left we pulled into the driveway of what had been my home for most of my adult life. While the place was a bit musty, even though the cleaning service had aired it out, Rose liked it from the start.

"Wow!" she said. "Angela really did a great job decorating. I've never lived in a house this nice." She pointed out a number of items as we walked through the place and asked if those were things I had added since Angela died. She didn't miss a one and she was delighted when we got to my study.

"This place is totally Ralph," she laughed and the first place we made love in our new home was on my ancient leather couch. We were lucky I had closed the front door and we had time to dress. A neighbor had seen us drive in and came a-knocking while the shack was a-rocking. Not that we fooled her a bit but we did have time to dress.

"The only thing I see we need to do is child proofing," Rose told me later. "But that's a long time off. The biggest decision right now is which room to use as a nursery."

"I thought we might use Angela's sewing room," I told her. "It's right next to the master bedroom."

"Are you sure?" Rose asked. "That would be more

convenient but we could leave it just the way it is for a guest room."

"No," I said. "Angie would like that. It was our daughter's room until she left home." Memory of the loss brought tears to my eyes.

"Are you sure you want to do this, Ralph? We don't have to live here. You could rent this place or sell it and we could find our own home."

I shook my head. "No, that would be foolish. I'm an old fart and I'm used to this place. I am really glad you don't mind living here. The years I was here alone I lived in the kitchen and in the basement."

"The basement is definitely male turf," she replied, nodding. "Was that where your son's room was?"

I laughed. "Yes, The basement was his cave but we all used the family room down there for TV. That's the only one in the house except for the small one in the kitchen. I would prefer not to have one in the bedroom, if you don't mind."

"I totally agree on that. Our bedroom is for sleeping and loving. It might be nice to have a set in the living room if we don't want to use the basement." She paused. "I also noticed a dog dish by the washing machine. Do you have one?"

"I did. He was a wonderful old mutt called Boswell, Boz for short. I lost him last fall. He was eighteen." I stopped and took a deep breath. "I'm sorry, Rose. I didn't realize there were so many memories with this place. Boz was my son's dog. We inherited him when Junior was killed."

"How long did you live here?"

"Over thirty years this summer. Most of my married life."

"So you've taught here more than thirty years? You could have retired, what, ten years ago?"

"Yes, but it just didn't work out. I stayed on because Angie was sick and we needed the health insurance. After that it was because I was so lonely. I almost sold the place and moved to Florida but I just couldn't get myself going. It was too easy just to stay here a little bit longer and after a while I got used to it." I looked at her and smiled. "Then I met this brown-eyed beauty from Texas and she blew me out of my rut."

Rose gave me an odd look when I said that and I quickly added, "For which I am eternally grateful. I think I was dying from the inside out. You and that little stranger in your womb have given me a good reason to live."

"God, Ralph. I had no idea. I'm glad I didn't know." Then she grinned. "On the other hand, you sure didn't show it. You swept me off my feet and knocked me up higher than a kite."

I laughed. "My recollection is that the sweeping of feet was rather mutual."

Rose's face became serious. "Well, since we're telling the truth, you've given me a good reason to live, too, Ralph. The truth is that I've been drifting for a long time, too. Going after my degree was marking time. Yes, I liked going back to school again, but it was mostly for a change. English was an easy major. I like to read and I like to do research but I had absolutely no idea what I was going to do after I got my master's. Going after a doctorate didn't interest me at all."

Suddenly I had one of those startling moments of clarity that happen from time to time. Yet I said nothing. I was rendered speechless, swept away in an overwhelming sense of presence as tangible as my encounter with the Dali crucifix.

Rose picked up on this immediately. "What's going on, Ralph?" she asked, clearly frightened.

I couldn't answer except to open my arms and hold her. We stood there for what seemed like a long while before I whispered, "Jesus! Was I ever wrong."

Rose pulled back and looked at me intently. "What are

you saying, Ralph? I don't understand. Were you wrong about us?"

"No, Rose," I assured her. "I am absolutely certain about us. I am also absolutely certain that Someone or Something is messing around in our lives and brought us together. How could I have been so blind?"

Taking her hand I led Rose into the living room, sitting down in a large easy chair and seating her in my lap. "You're very right, my love," I told her. "I have lived all my life in my mind. It was my way of trying to control my life and to make sense of things. Up to a point it worked. Then it didn't. The kids were killed in a car wreck and I think that's when Angela gave up hope. She kept up a brave front and agreed to surgery and chemo at first, but I think she did that for me. I was Mister Power-of-positive-thinking-we're-going-to-kick-this-thing-in-the-ass. I'm beginning to see just how wrong I was. That was my plan, not hers, but I wasn't listening and she never accepted more than palliative pain management. Up to the time the kids died, she was anything but a quitter."

I stopped but Rose must have known I wasn't finished. She didn't say a word. She simply wrapped me in her arms and surrounded me with compassion. After a few moments I was able to continue.

"What happened just now was another moment of clarity, Rose. I just realized how living in my head led me down a long, blind alley. It's pretty obvious how little control I have over anything. It's an illusion but it wasn't my mind that convinced me of that. It was my heart. I can't believe how blind I've been."

Rose frowned. "I understand what you're telling me, lover, but I can't see how bashing yourself will help. I think you may need to respond some other way. Tell me, are you grateful for knowing this now?"

"God, yes! I wish it had been sooner, but I'm grateful it happened at all."

"Maybe you weren't ready to learn this before now."

"That's scary. I have no idea what's coming next. If I don't make things happen, who will?"

"Let me approach it another way. Do you trust what you're learning?"

I looked into the eyes of my bride. There was nothing there but goodness. "That's a strange question. I think I can...no, I feel like I can. It's just so foreign to how I've been taught to meet the world. What are you getting at?"

"Well, if you can trust what you've learned, can't you trust whomever is teaching you? Don't answer that with your head. Answer that from the heart."

"You're boxing me in," I told her. "What you say feels right, so right it makes me want to run."

"I'm not talking to just you, Ralph. I'm hearing what I'm saying and it scares me spitless, too. I am as clueless as you are about this stuff. That's even though I've seen it over and over working in the ER and the ICU, the intensive care unit. There are a lot of people walking around who by all odds should have died but didn't."

"So what do we do?"

Rose shook her head and smiled. "I don't know about you but your brat is telling me he or she is hungry." Then she grew serious again. "I think we just live life as best we can and when these things happen we thank Whomever It May Concern and go on. If you think about it, that's about all we can do, anyway. It won't help driving ourselves crazy."

Rose paused and I knew she had more to say. "You're an English teacher, Ralph. Have you ever come across the work of Francis Thompson?"

"The name rings a bell but I can't place it," I replied.

"What he's most famous for is an epic poem called The *Hound of Heaven*. It was very well known in his lifetime."

"Of course! The analogy is right on target. I even know part of it by heart." I thought for a moment and began to speak.

> I fled Him, down the nights and down the days;
> I fled Him, down the arches of the years;
> I fled Him, down the labyrinthine ways
> Of my own mind; and in the mist of tears....

Rose looked at me oddly. "You're sure mystical for someone who claims to be an agnostic."

The observation surprised me. "Why do you say that?"

My question surprised her as much as she had me. "For goodness sake, Ralph. Think about the small part of your life I've seen so far. Who was it who was almost driven to his knees by encountering a crucifix? Who told me about his sense of a Presence at Saint Patrick's and told me about having experienced that in other holy places? Who went back to Saint Pat's and passed out in the chapel later that same day? Who seems to know his way around the Rosary and can quote Francis Thompson?"

Rose shook her head. "I'm convinced the reason the doctors couldn't find anything wrong with you is because there's nothing wrong to find."

"You think I was faking it?" I was shocked at the suggestion, indignant.

"Of course, not, silly man! I am saying you are a very spiritual fellow and that doesn't usually go with being an agnostic. Not from what I've seen."

"All that 'agnostic' means is that I don't know the answers, Rose. The word comes from the Greek word for knowledge, gnosis. Tacking an alpha on the front of it means 'no knowledge, *agnosis.*' Or as I tell my students, it means I have no for-sure answers."

Rose refused to be deflected. "That night I locked the bedroom door, where did you go?"

I was surprised. "I went out to the place where we sometimes had coffee."

"Yes, but I sat there for a long time before I spoke to you. You didn't seem to know I was there. Where were you right then?"

"I called it the Void and later on, the Abyss. The Void was a safe place I learned to go as a child when the abuse got so bad I couldn't stand any more. It's gotten me through a lot of bad times ever since. I could check out and not feel the awful things that were going on in my life. The big thing about it is that there weren't any questions I had to answer, and nothing was required of me except to simply be. Later I ran into the writing of a fourteenth century mystic who called this the Cloud of Unknowing. His idea was to use spiritual discipline to get rid of all our preconceptions and to enter a state of unknowing where we can begin to comprehend the actual nature of God."

"Why do you call it the Abyss now? That's from Nietzsche, isn't it?"

"Yes, from *Beyond Good and Evil.* He wrote that those who fight monsters need to take care they do not become monsters themselves. That when we stare into the Abyss long enough, the Abyss stares back. At that point I thought the Abyss was the place where my personal demons dwell."

"At that point? Where do you think they dwell now?"

"They're probably still there but I don't see them as demons any more. I see them as angels waiting to be born. A very wise priest once told me that. The problem is that he went on to say that for this to happen we have to turn them over to the tender mercies of Whomever may or may not be there. That's scary."

Rose nodded. "I came across something like that in my research. It's a poem written in the mid 'seventies. It was called Faith. It goes something like this."

Rose paused a moment and began to speak so softly I almost could barely hear what she was saying. "When our path leads us to the end of the light we are given and we step off into the darkness that lies ahead, we must have faith that one of two things will occur. Either there will be a path there for our feet to follow, or we will discover we have grown wings."

"Yes. Wasn't that written by a nuclear physicist, one of the ones who helped develop the atomic bomb? Edward something or other."

"Edward Teller," Rose said, smiling. "No, though he's been given credit. That makes a good story but it's been attributed to a lot of other people, too. It was first published in a collection called *The Leaning Tree* by Patrick Overton."

"You never cease to amaze me, Rose," I told her. "I know I've told you that before but every time I do it's even more so. Thank you for sharing your life with me."

Rose looked at me with a raised eyebrow. It seemed to stretch almost to her normal hairline. "Pashaw, mistuh Cody Adams. You just trying to get in my payunts."

"Seriously, Rose, I mean it."

She look at me intently. "I know, Ralph, but it still scares me sometimes. Just hold me for a while." Then she giggled. "Just hold us. "I'm still getting used to the idea of that, too."

"We have several months to get used to it, my love. Just so you know, I'd like to have another one right away, too. As soon as you're healthy enough."

"You planning to keep me barefoot and pregnant, mister?"

"Good heavens, no. Not barefoot, not in Minnesota. It gets cold here. Come to think, not in Texas either. Too many grass burrs and far-aints. Them thangs really stang."

"But pregnant?"

"Barkis is willing," I told her and she laughed.

"One child at a time, husband. One child at a time."

6

North Home

A couple of weeks after we arrived in Minnesota a couple from the University hosted a party to celebrate our arrival. It was held at their family home on the lake on a Saturday afternoon. The weather could not have been better and Rose was an immediate hit with my friends on the faculty. Most of these folk were about the same age as she, though few of them had young children. The exception was a close friend of mine, an earthy soul in his late forties with a tiny firebrand for a wife and six children to prove it. "Goodness," Rose said when I told her how many. "I can't imagine having so many. Are they Roman Catholic?"

"Why don't you ask him," I suggested, knowing exactly what Tony would say. Rose looked at me as if I had grown an extra head. "Really, he won't mind your asking. Not at all," I assured her.

Rose looked at me, clearly skeptical. "You're up to something," she said but after a while I saw her talking to the man and I moved close enough to eavesdrop. "It's none of my business," she said, "but I was just wondering...."

Tony chuckled. "You were wondering whether we're Catholics, having so many kids." Rose nodded and the room suddenly got quiet just as Tony answered. Everyone was watching. "No, Rose, we're not Catholic. We're just careless Protestants."

Everyone laughed though they'd seen the same performance many times before. It was almost a rite of passage in that crowd.

"You turkey!" Rose growled quietly a few minutes later when we were alone. "You're just asking for it, Buster. Wait until I get you home."

"We could slip upstairs," I offered. She answered with a discreet goose that made me jump.

I was about to take her up on this but someone latched onto me wanting to talk about a study she had just come across. I can't remember what it was or even what it was about, but compared to a tryst with Rose, what can I say? When they were growing up my kids would have described the woman as Totally Bo-ring, the greatest deadly sin to an adolescent.

To be honest, I think the interjector was miffed by my lack of interest. I know she was jealous of Rose. Two months after Angela died the woman had made a play for me and I turned her down flat. There was nothing I found attractive about her, personally or professionally, aside from her absence. Yet I was polite at the time and tried to let her down gently. This may have been a mistake. She had gone on the attack, spreading malicious lies about me.

However, Lars and Mary, our hosts, are far more charitable than I. They felt sorry for Letitia and I think she knew this and took advantage. I often wondered how they would feel if either of them had been the target of the vituperative gossip that had gotten back about me. I wondered why Letitia would even want to be at the party but I suspect it was to gather dirt for gossip.

Fortunately the dean happened by just then and wanted to know how I was doing. Rose had him wrapped around her little finger in fifteen seconds flat and our *coitus iterpellator* wandered off to refill her wine glass. Nor did she offer to fetch a fresh one for any of us.

Rose, of course, had picked up on my feelings and asked

me about them on the way home. I explained what had happened. "I'm not sure I understand what's going on with Latitia," I said. "I have never given her any encouragement but she won't back off. It's been that way since the day she arrived. I seem to be her personal challenge and she refuses to understand. It's tempting to tell her I wouldn't take her to a dogfight even if she promised to win."

Rose laughed. "That's probably not a good idea, lover. That would only give her more ammo to use against you. You do realize she's going to attack both of us with anything she can, don't you?"

I nodded. "Yes, but I think my friends will stand by us. My retirement may help. Out of sight out of mind and if worse comes to worse, I know where the bodies are buried."

Rose looked at me sharply. "I'm not sure I like the sound of that. What do you mean?"

"It means I'll do about anything to protect you and our child," I told her. I turned my head and looked at her. "I don't think what she's up to will go beyond gossip. Even that may backfire on her."

"How's that?"

"Letitia comes up for tenure this fall. I'm on the committee and my retirement does not begin officially until after the first of the year. Even as a lame loon I probably have the clout to swing the vote against her. That would be the third strike and she would have to move on."

"That sounds drastic, Ralph. Why would you want to do that? Revenge can come back to bite you. It's not like you, either."

I nodded. "So I'm told. Should I decide to vote against her, it will be for the good of the university. I owe a lot to this place and she is no asset. Quite the contrary."

We were late getting home that night, late being almost

midnight. I tend to be a morning sort and have always been. Most of the time I am asleep by ten and up by seven, eight at the latest. Nor do I snap back from a late night the way I once did. I remember a professor once telling us that we require less sleep as we age and I suppose I haven't reached the magic age yet. One would think so at three score and a half, but then I've always done things a bit differently. This is no longer deliberate. These days I don't chouse others for the sport of it, and I suspect being disparate has become a habit of soul. Yet I don't apologize for marching to the beat of a different drummer or being who I am.

Rose was up when I wandered into the kitchen. We were still unpacking and she was trying to figure out where things needed to go. I had lived with the current arrangement for many years and was comfortable with that. Even so, I had given her carte blanche with the place and she had claimed the kitchen as her special domain. At some point she had mentioned going to culinary school in passing and took creating our meals quite seriously. Nor could I argue with the result. My palate might not be as well developed as hers, but the things she came up with were works of art. At least, they were to me and our occasional guests seemed to think so, too.

The interesting thing about that first summer together was that we seemed to have a lot of company. Angela and I had always had a lot of drop-in visitors until the kids were killed but that had tapered off a few weeks after their funeral. It picked up again briefly after she had been diagnosed but she was not very welcoming at that point. There were only three of her long time friends that continued to visit almost every week and each of them brought a casserole. I believe they thought I'd starve if they didn't.

They may have been right. Eating at that point was nothing

to me but fueling the machine and there were times I forgot to eat. Then, when the organism demanded nutrients, I'd devour half a casserole at a sitting. These were disgustingly healthy, full of stuff things like broccoli and cauliflower I normally detest. Yet with enough cheese sauce or catsup I could usually choke most things down and I discovered a taste for Sweet Baby Ray's barbecue sauce. It made Spam and hard boiled eggs edible when I craved fat and protein.

"So what are you mulling about, big guy?" Rose asked, pulling me back to the here and now.

I woke up, realizing I was standing at the kitchen sink staring at the lake, focused on nothing. I had a dish in one hand and a bowl in the other and I realized I had paused half way between wash and rinse.

"Spam," I replied, rinsing the bowl and setting it on the rack.

"That's not what we had for breakfast," she reminded me. "Did you want it for lunch? Or were you thinking about unwanted email?"

I had to smile. "It was a staple for me after Angela died. I bought it by the case. It was fast and easy and I could even eat it right out of the can."

"Yuck! Do you have any idea what it did to your arteries?"

"I think the broccoli evened things out," I told her. She looked puzzled and I told her about all the casseroles our friends brought. "I think it must be in the Minnesota constitution somewhere. Thou shalt not make casserole without broccoli, cauliflower, green beans, or asparagus. You'll see. When the first funeral happens, check out the potluck offering at the meal afterward."

"Are you expecting someone to die?" she asked.

"No but who knows? I've lived here so long that I know most of the people in the obits. Most of the rest I know second hand. One way or another I'm only two or three degrees separated from almost everyone in this area and I attend a lot of funerals. Most of the people I know were students of mine."

"Would they tell me you were a hard-ass as a teacher, or an old softie?" There was a glint of challenge in her eyes.

"Those going for an A will tell you I was a real hard-ass. On the other hand, it was almost impossible to fail. Those who did had to work at it. It was actually easier to get an A."

"So you didn't grade on the curve?"

"Are you trying to piss me off?" I asked, smiling. "Those who grade on the curve are the strongest argument I know for capital punishment. "

Rose gave me a stern look. "Seriously, Ralph. What's wrong with it?"

"According to me, it's inherently unfair. It promotes mediocrity, as well. The bell shaped curve is a statistical tool for describing a large population of things or events. It may be useful looking at class grades over a decade or two to determine trends, but what about an unusually bright class? What if you don't have a single C level student in the class? Are you going to punish highly competent A and B level students by forcing thirty or forty percent of them to accept a C?"

"It cuts the other way, too," Rose insisted. "Too many A's in one semester waters the achievement down."

"How? It's the rigid adherence to a curve that does that. What if you have a class of less gifted students, all C level? Are you going to give thirty to forty percent of them an A or a B just to satisfy the prediction curve? The curve is a research tool, not an academic canon."

Suddenly, I realized how I must sound. "Sorry for the soapbox sermon. It's a sore point with me."

"Yes, it apparently is. How about a back rub to help you relax."

"You're just trying to get me in the sack."

"No, husband, I'm trying to get you wherever I can."

One day we were standing in our living room talking about how we might make it more comfortable when Rose took down a family photo from the mantle. It was one I had taken using the shutter delay and we were all there, the two of us with our grown children and our only grandchild. "Are these your children?" she asked. I thought she had probably noticed the photo right away the day we arrived but this was the first time she asked.

"Yes," I answered. "That was taken about a month before they died. That's our lake here in the background."

"Do you mind my asking how they passed?"

"I understand why people use euphemisms, my love, but I prefer more direct language when it comes to the big things." I smiled to take any sting out of my words. "People and other creatures die. Gas passes."

"I'm sorry. I didn't mean to be nosy."

"No, there's no need to apologize. I don't mind your questions at all. It's all part of my history and the more you know, the better. I can talk about it now. There was a time I couldn't. I don't know how I ever got through those first few months."

Rose was silent and I realized I had not answered her question. "It was a collision with a train. The car they were driving was completely smashed, literally torn apart. Junior and his sister, Carol, were driving up from the Cities together with their families. All of them were together in a minivan and they were coming up for Angela's birthday. It turned out there was something wrong with the crossing signal. The lights didn't come on and the arm didn't drop. It was a blind crossing, too, heavily wooded and on a sharp curve. No one saw the train coming until it was too late. The car right behind them was barely able to stop in time."

"How awful!" Rose said, reaching out to touch my face. I felt myself choking and couldn't reply. "I'm sorry I asked," she added.

"Don't be. It was awful," I told her when I caught my breath. "As you can imagine, it had to be a closed casket funeral. The funeral director told me it was impossible telling who was who except for the baby. That was the one that hit us the hardest."

I paused and Rose waited patiently and I told myself to keep breathing. After a bit I was able to continue. "The crash destroyed Angela's will to live. The cancer that actually killed her was diagnosed less than a year later, but there were early symptoms six months before the diagnosis. Angela refused to see doctor until it was far too late and she refused treatment, too. Six weeks later she was dead. I have often wondered if she knew how sick she was from the start. For a while I was very angry at her for leaving me in the lurch." I shrugged. "It took me a long time to get beyond that.

Rose was quiet for a moment. "So you lost your whole family within what, a year and a half?"

"Closer to two years. Angela died two weeks before her birthday." I sighed. "It took me a long time to forgive her for being so pig-headed. Now I understand she was doing the best she could."

"You do know that pancreatic cancer has a very low survival rate, don't you?"

"Later on it does. If it is caught early enough it has a hell of a lot greater survival rate. It's at least a fighting chance but she didn't fight it. Her life ended with that crash." I took a deep breath and let it out slowly.

"So what about Ralph?" Rose asked. "What about his will to live?"

I tried to deflect my feelings with humor but my jest came out as a raw croak, almost a scream. "Rose, my will to live died when I was a child. My parents abused me in about every way a child can be abused. I have only talked with one other survivor who had it worse than me. Her earliest memory is being offered up as a live sacrifice and being left to die on a stone altar. To this day she can't stand anything that sounds like beating drums."

"Yes, but what about you, Ralph?"

"I guess I'm lucky to have been spared that. The worst part of my abuse was the shaming. My parents would violate me sexually and then shame me for being seductive when I sought love or attention. They punished me for doing exactly what they taught me to do to be loved. I had no way of knowing how wrong they were. Or how much pain this would cause me and other people I cared about later on before I understood how wrong they were."

Rose started to say something but shook her head and I went on. "I remember being terrified, Rose. I remember dreaming someone was chasing me in order to hurt me and not being able to run away. That memory is almost seventy years old. I must have been three or four when it happened. I can even remember what I was wearing and the bed I was in like it was yesterday."

I walked over to the plate glass window that overlooked the lake and sat on the couch put there for viewing. When I held out my hand, Rose came with me and sat close. "I've always found that sitting here calms me down," I told her. I lifted an arm and she snuggled close.

"I've got more to tell you but let's be quiet for a bit," I asked her.

"We don't have to do this now, Ralph. Or ever if you don't want," she answered.

"No, the worst was what I told you, the shaming. The result is that I was suicidal as a teen. I took awful risks and there wasn't much I wouldn't try. I was also so angry nobody else wanted to be around me for long and that only fed my sense of being a piece of shit. That happens a lot to survivors I'm told."

"Some of that's still true of you, Ralph. The risk taking. Not in a bad way, but it's still there."

"What makes you say that?" I wanted to know.

Rose smiled. "Are you kidding? Think about what I've seen you do." She counted with her fingers. "The first thing I saw was that awesome emotional risk you took being so open at the conference. I have never seen anyone allow himself to be so vulnerable with a group of strangers. Then you went to bed with a woman you didn't know and took absolutely no precautions against an STD or conception. You could have knocked her up that first night. Then you didn't bother taking any precautions and you did impregnate her. Then you married her not having known her more than a few weeks and you opened your home and your circle of friends to her."

I couldn't help smiling at all that. "When you put it that way, it does seem risky. It sure didn't seem so at the time. The only things I was afraid of was your ridiculing such a pathetic old turkey and walking out the door. You have no idea how awful that night you got back from Austin was for me. I was convinced I had somehow made a mess of the best thing that ever happened to me."

Rose shook her head and smiled. "You sure have your head wedged for such an intelligent man, Ralph. So what got you turned around? When you were a teen?"

I thought for a moment. "Leaving home," I told her.

"Getting out of that toxic environment was the first step although I carried it with me for a long while. I still do, apparently. Anyway, I did well in high school and qualified for a full-ride scholarship at a major university. That covered tuition, books, and a little left over for incidentals. The Dean of Students also helped me find a good part-time job to cover room and board and that job carried me through to graduation three years later." I stopped for a moment.

"Then during my first semester an English teacher told me I wrote well so that's what I chose for a major. It was incredible being around people who admired my intellect and ability to write. I was amazed when my first novel became a best seller the winter before I graduated, and that helped me find my way into an MFA program." I chuckled, remembering.

"Even so, I wondered how in the world I had managed to fool everyone so long and I didn't quit my part-time job. I was afraid someone had made a mistake and that I'd have to give all the money back. So I put it in the bank and saved every bit."

Rose laughed. "Seriously?" she asked.

"Seriously," I told her. "I didn't think my first book was all that good. Or the second, either. I only discovered that when I read them again many years later. They were damned good."

Rose nodded. "So what kept you going through the bad times?"

"At first it was proving to myself that I wasn't the piece of shit my dad said I was. Looking back, he never called me that in so many words, but the physical abuse and his indifference conveyed the idea quite well. He also played all kinds of mind games but there was never any question I would never prove myself in his eyes. So I stopped trying and began trying to prove him right. Not consciously, but in the stupid choices I made. I'm surprised I didn't end up in reform school or prison."

"I have a little trouble believing that," Rose told me. "What did you do?"

"Back then it was called pranks. Now it would be seen as terroristic acts. A buddy of mine and I liked to put together home made hand grenades and blow stuff up. The last time we did it we blew the door off a house and we realized we could have killed somebody. Thank God we didn't."

"Thank God you didn't get caught, either."

Then I had a thought that made me laugh. "You want to know the real irony, Rose? The irony is that I chose to be dirt poor. My dad had a very good job and could have afforded to send me to college, especially with my scholarship. I didn't even ask. I knew what he would do if I put myself in his power. He would have wanted to control every choice I had and I would have never become a successful writer. An MBA would have been his choice and he would have made me beg for every cent he gave me. Nor would he have accepted my being anything but at the very top of my class."

"So the irony is that you became a success on your own terms?"

"No, for me the irony is that my poverty was responsible for my success as a writer. I was so busy working and going to school that I didn't have the time or the money to do anything but study and write. So I had my first book written by the end of my second year in college. It started as a simple love story about two young people of different races, but ended up being about growing up in the South during the integration wars. That's why I wrote it under a pen name. I could have been shot for what I had to say if anyone knew who I was. Arkansas was on the front lines and feelings on campus were very intense."

"Is that when you met Angela?"

"Yes, during my first week there but she only attended the first semester. With all the strife on campus, her family brought her home. I never understood why until I met them some time later. Angela was as light skinned as I am but she let me know right away that she had relatives who were colored folk, as she put it. She also let me know it was not a subject for discussion so I didn't ask about it. That was a very touchy issue back then. Arkansas had abandoned the standard one-eighth rule and operated under the one drop law. So I assumed her colored relatives were in-laws."

Rose nodded and I continued. "Then that first summer she told me she wanted me to meet her parents. We had been writing back and forth all year and it was pretty obvious how we both felt by then but I didn't have a clue what to expect when I showed up in Dallas. You can imagine my surprise when I met her father. Not only was he clearly a person of color, he was a preacher and well known in the civil rights movement. He was not pleased to meet me, either."

"'I gather my daughter hasn't told you about us,' he observed seeing my reaction. When he spoke it was with the voice of God and he was aware of the effect he had."

"No, sir," I told him. "She has not but I am pleased to meet you, despite the fact you're a Baptist preacher. I think we're probably all right as long as we don't talk about religion."

I smiled at the memory. "Angela looked like she was about to faint and it hung in the balance for a long moment. Then her father chuckled and extended his hand and I knew it was all right. 'Indeed,' he chuckled. 'That's probably wise. I take it you are not one.'

"Even if I were, sir, there are at least two hundred varieties of those."

"'Now isn't that right?" he agreed. "I think it's a good measure of our sinfulness.'

"I'm not wise enough to make that determination, sir."

"The reverend chuckled again. He seemed to be reluctant to release my hand. 'Yes, there is that. Well, come in, please. Take a chair.' He pointed to a well seasoned rocker not unlike the one used by our late President."

"Who was he?" Rose wanted to know. I mentioned a name and she blinked. "Wasn't he one of the ones who was killed?"

"No, but he was shot and badly wounded. He lived to be an old man and it was he who performed the ceremony when Angela and I married."

"Wow," Rose said. "So was it your courtship with Angela that inspired *Blood Ties*?"

"It was but that's privileged information. As far as the world knows, it was pure invention. That was my agreement with Angela. She was a very private person and not even our children knew. The truth is that a lot of my material came directly out of our relationship."

Rose reflected on all I had told her. "I think you mentioned at the conference that writing was a form of therapy for you."

"It was a safe way to come to terms with my demons but it wasn't the only form of therapy I made use of over the years. I've had several counselors and a lot of good friends, too. I go to week long retreats from time to time, too."

"You mean religious retreats?"

"No, spiritual retreats, mostly with other men. A lot of them are in recovery and a lot of them suffered the same kind of abuse I did. So we talk about these things and sweat the poison out in the sweat-lodge, but there are some fun things we do, too. We tell stories and play the drums and sometimes we even sing and dance. There's a lot of gentle humor, too."

We sat there quietly for a long time. After a time Rose said, "This is very nice, being together like this."

"It's one of my favorite ways we make love," I told her, giving her a hug. "It's so much better than looking into the Abyss."

Rose looked up at me and smiled. I realized once again how good it is to be looked at that way. "Are we feeling urgent or are you up to a couple more questions?" she asked.

"I'm actually feeling kind of lazy at the moment. Very mellow, too. Ask away."

"I was wondering about your MFA. Someone I talked to before we met told me that there are two versions to your second book. Is that right?"

"Yes, that's right," I told her. "Do you want the down and dirty version or the official one?"

"Down and dirty," she laughed. "I probably have the sanitized version."

"All right. The d-and-d truth is that having a best seller before I graduated got me into a prestigious MFA program in the midwest. Yet, in some ways it was a real liability. I didn't realize this at the time but there were a number of faculty in the department that wanted nothing to do with me. This was made clear to me the first week I was there. Fool that I was, I thought I could win over my adversaries and I tried. Yet they were cast in the same mold as my dad. The harder I tried to prove myself, the more abusive they became. It was only through the support of a strong department chair and three powerful faculty members that I was ever approved for the degree. Were you aware of that?"

"No, not at all. Do you know why they were so set against you?"

"The only thing I could figure was simple jealousy. There were three of them and very single one of them was a failed novelist. They were all published but their books had not sold worth a damn. None of them had been able to get a manuscript accepted after their first. All of them held a PhD in American literature and every single one had spent most of their carriers teaching English 101. They were tenured by the time the MFA program started and each of them wormed their way onto the MFA faculty. Fortunately, one of them was on sabbatical the year I graduated and the other two were simply outvoted. Later the department chairman told me it was their abuse of me that enabled him to force all three out. He said the program really took off after that."

"How awful!" Rose said, indignant.

"Yes, but surely you've heard the old saw that nothing bad ever happens to a writer."

Rose smiled. "Yes, it's all material. But you didn't answer my question. Why were there two versions of *Arm of the Lord*?"

"One was the original version as it came of my typewriter, which my publisher really liked and bought. It was also the version I submitted to my thesis committee. The second is the revised version that was finally accepted by that same committee on a four to two vote. Normally their approval would require a unanimous vote but the chairman managed to get that waived. This set a precedent which came back to haunt him but that was the price of getting the deadwood out of the department."

"All right, but it's the revised manuscript that ended up being printed and went on to become a best seller like the first, isn't it? How did that happen?"

"My publisher heard about the revision and asked to see it. I showed it to him and he liked it much better. He said it was a better manuscript and I was already under contract. So I agreed to let him make the changes and it was a commercial success. When I compared the two versions many years later, I had to agree."

"What are you smiling about?" Rose asked.

"Oh, my publisher was retired by then but I wrote him a letter and told him he was right. He thought that was pretty funny. We had argued about it for all those years so he phoned to give me a hard time about it. He's gone now, died last year. Damn, I miss him! He was a good friend."

"Yes, I really enjoyed visiting with him."

"How did you know him?" I wanted to know.

"I did my research and gave him a call for background. He invited me to visit him in the care center and we had a delightful visit. He spoke very highly of you."

"I guess I had him fooled," I said, remembering our many visits over the year.

"Now stop that," Rose commanded gently. "Stand up and take your medicine like a man."

I looked down at her and decided a thorough kiss was in order. "You're my medicine, woman," I told her.

"Goodness, stud muffin," she answered, smiling, and kissed me again. "From zero to urgent in one second flat."

Later that afternoon we were looking at the lake again. After a long quiet time Rose asked if I would mind giving her more personal background. "Sure," I told her. "All I ask is that you ask me before you use it. So far you haven't asked anything I would object to your using it."

"It's not so much for my thesis," she told me. "I'm concerned about the suicide issue, Ralph. You've been through so much. What's kept you alive?"

I though for a long moment. "I used to wonder that, myself. For a long while it was keeping a lid on what was going on inside. That didn't work very well and I'm told it never does. The issue was not anger. It was rage and that came out sideways, as one counselor put it. I would get too angry over what would normally be trivial stuff. Growing up as she did, Angela was very well acquainted with rage and she was pretty effective dealing with her own feelings. So was her dad and, oddly enough, he helped me quite a bit."

"What was odd about it?"

"Mostly that he was my father-in-law. We had to be very careful about the boundaries and some subjects were not for discussion. Dealing with rage was one thing. My relationship with Angela was another, as was religion. He also put me in touch with a very wise older minister who helped incredibly. He was mentor for a lot of the black preachers in the movement and he is the least judgmental man I ever met. He was very helpful helping me see what was most important and in putting first things first. He also put me in touch with a lot of the men in the movement. Those men provided so much material for my third novel that I had a hard time deciding what to use. A lot of them really liked what I had to say in the first two and others were surprised to learn I was a white man."

Rose looked thoughtful. "Your third book? You mean *Buffalo Mountain*? That wasn't about the civil right movement."

"No, it was about the Japanese interment in Cody, Wyoming during the second world war. That was the third one actually published but *Scraggin' the Dragon* was the third one I wrote. My publisher held it back because he was afraid I'd be shot. There was a lot of that still going on in the South back then."

I laughed. "I'm lucky he took the long view. Having me shot would have boosted sales."

Rose ignored my jest. "I can see why he was scared," she declared. "You took on the Ku Klux Klan head to head and you made it very clear you weren't writing fiction. You damn near named names and you had the proof to back it up. People have been shot for a lot less, Ralph."

"I wasn't that concerned, Rose. I had already taken on the CSA with *Arm of the Lord* and they were a lot more dangerous than the Klan, mostly because they were better organized. We had moved to Minnesota not long before and my dust jackets identified me as being from the South, which was true. I grew up there. I also kept a very low profile as a writer. When I had to do publicity appearances I couldn't avoid, I wore thick horn rim glasses with coke bottle lenses and a fake beard. I think I still have those around here some place. I also wore a couple of really dorky sport jackets and a couple of ugly fish ties that were my trademark, along with my white socks. All those accoutrements went to Good Will a long time ago."

Rose didn't say a word. She didn't have to. The look on her face told me she thought I was full of caca and I knew nothing I could say would convince her otherwise. "You must have had some interesting family gatherings," she said. "How did your family react?"

"I was totally cut off from my family of origin. I used to send my mother cards at Christmas and Easter, and on her birthday. I was very careful to avoid giving her any personal information at all. Her letters back were always an attempt to heap guilt on my head. So after a while I stopped reading them. I did go back for my father's funeral, but I went alone. Our children were still in school and had never met my parents. Since I didn't have siblings there weren't any nieces or nephews and the only family at the funeral were some of my mother's cousins I had never met. It was sad but with my dad being the way he was...." I shrugged.

Rose snuggled closer. "You know, I'd really rather talk

about you," I told her. "I don't think I'm all that interesting."

"Right,"she murmured. Then she looked at me and grinned. "I think it's time for a nap."

"Good. That's exactly what I was thinking, too."

After supper that evening we sat by the open fire. It wasn't all that cold but a front had moved through shedding a world of rain and giving us mild weather for that time of year. After a long silence I turned to my bride and said, "I feel a need to clarify something, Rose. I don't want you to worry about me."

She looked at me, clearly puzzled. "You asked me how I got through the dark times," I reminded her. "I think you were concerned about me being suicidal and I never gave you a good answer. I need to reassure you that's not an option."

"You don't have to tell me anything more than you did, Ralph. I'm here if you need to talk about it but I'm not worried."

"I didn't think you were but I'd like to tell you why. Have you ever watched Bill Murray in Groundhog Day?"

"Only about thirty times," she replied, smiling. "I don't know why but it's one of my favorite movies."

I nodded. "Me, too. It's all about karma. Phil keeps trying make things come out the way he wants, but every morning he wakes up at the exact same time of the day he lived yesterday. Only nothing ever turns out right for him until he surrenders and lives the day the way he is supposed to live. There is no escape, not even suicide, which he tries in several ways. He keeps on having to do the same old day over and over again until he gets it right. Are you with me so far?"

Rose nodded and I continued. "Well, that's how it is for me. What kept me from pulling the plug in even the most rotten times was the odd notion that if I did commit suicide, I might have to come back and do this same life over and over again until I finally got it right."

Rose laughed when I said this, then tried to apologize. "You don't need to apologize, Rose," I told her. "That's how most people I've ever told about it react. The idea is so absurd it's hard to take seriously. The thing is, since the very moment I had this thought, suicide has never been an option."

"For real?" she asked.

I nodded. "With a family I had a reason to live. Then for many years after Angela died, I had my work and my students. Those all gave me a strong reason to keep going and I dreaded retirement. That would have left me with no reason to stay alive. Now you and the little stranger you are carrying have given me another strong reason to keep going."

"What if something happens to us?" Rose asked. "Like it did to your wife and children."

"My father-in-law would have quoted Scripture," I told her, smiling. "He would have said, 'Sufficient unto the day is the evil thereof.'"

Rose nodded. "I'm glad people don't talk that way any more. I prefer 'We'll cross that bridge when we get to it.'"

"I used to know where that comes from," I told her. "I know it's not Billy the Bard."

"No, it's Henry Longfellow, from *The Golden Legend*. According to him it was already an English proverb."

"Wow. You'd have gotten an A in my classes."

"Yeah, but I sleep with the prof," Rose answered. "Speaking of which...."

"'Yes, yes, a thousand times yes.'" I replied.

"Now that one's easy. Jane Austen from *Pride and Prejudice*."

"You really are working for an A, aren't you?"

"You damn betchum, Red Ryder," she shot back. "That's why they call me Little Beaver."

7

Gospel Choir

We had a busy fall that first year we spent together. A lot of this was simply getting Rose acquainted with the people there. These were not just my friends on the faculty, but also the people I had traded with for years in town. My impression was that they gave Rose a warm welcome but she was a little concerned at first.

"The people I met are friendly enough," she told me. "but they seemed very reserved to me."

"This is actually their version of a very warm welcome," I assured her. "Remember, a lot of this state was settled by Norwegians. They may have a lot going on inside but they don't share it, especially with people they're meeting for the first time. Once you get to know them, it can be frightening just how intense they can be. The Swedes and the Germans tend to be a lot more relaxed and outgoing."

"Even on the faculty?" she asked.

"That's still true. There's a very low turnover rate on the university faculty here and a lot of them are former students and native Minnesotans. Look at the school annuals and you'll see what I mean."

"So how do I come across to these people? I hope I haven't offended anyone."

"You scare some of them spitless," I told her. "Most of them seem to find you very attractive."

"Right, having swallowed a pumpkin seed and all. I'm sure they can do the math."

"Yes, but these are farm people, too. They know how things are. They're used to brides getting a head start with a family. That's how some people get engaged."

"Like us, you mean," Rose replied, frowning. She looked doubtful.

"Seriously, Rose. A lot of the faculty are the first in their families to have gone to college or to graduate school and education is valued around here. So you probably have a lot more in common with most of the people you'll meet than you think."

"A couple of the women asked where we intended to go to church," Rose told me. "They were very polite about it but the assumption was that we would. I told them we hadn't decided that yet."

"That's a good answer. I haven't really been active since Angela died."

"What did you do about your children when they were growing up? Did you belong to a church?"

I had to laugh. "Are you kidding? With the in-laws I had? Not belonging was not an option. Even so, Angela did surprise me about that. Having been a Baptist preacher's kid she wanted nothing to do with evangelical religion, so we became Episcopalians. Her folks didn't like it but they came to accept it. So our kids were raised 'whiskey-palians' as my father-in-law liked to say. We also did well with the local padre. He had not been here long when the kids were killed and he was a pillar of strength through that. Then Angie was diagnosed with cancer and he was very helpful to us through the whole thing. He also helped me to keep going afterward. Then he left a year later and I just drifted away. I'm not sure I met the next priest."

"I don't know much about that church," Rose said. "Tell me about it."

I laughed, remembering. "The padre who we liked so well used to tell people it was Catholic light: all the same sacraments and half the guilt."

"I see why you liked him," Rose nodded. "Tell me more."

"I don't know a lot about it," I confessed. "What little I knew is mostly forgotten. Back when the kids were little I became a nominal member to support their spiritual education, but it was Angela who really carried the ball. What I saw, I liked, but I never got around to being baptized and the padre didn't push the issue. He even gave me communion at Angela's funeral though he wasn't supposed to do that."

Suddenly a memory broke through and punched me squarely in the solar plexus. It hit so hard I gasped and had to sit down. Rose was on her feet in a half second, checking my pulse and asking me what I was feeling. It was all I could do to answer.

"A memory," I gasped. "It was something I can't believe I forgot. I'm sorry. It all makes sense now. Give me a minute."

Rose waited patiently, watching me closely, like a cat spotting a mouse. Later she told me it was the longest seven minutes of her life.

"I need to explain something that never made sense to me before. It was when the kids were confirmed. I was there when old padre explained to them what it meant to take communion. He had no idea I had not been baptized and I didn't realize you had to do that to be a member of the church."

I closed my eyes and recalled the face of that gentle old man. "He told them that when a priest says mass, something happens to the bread and the wine. The Roman Catholics believe they become the body and blood of Christ, literally. He told us that Anglicans believe in something called Real Presence. What that means is that while the bread and wine stay bread and wine, somehow Christ becomes present in them in a very special way. He went on to say it doesn't really matter which of these we believe. What happens is that when we take the consecrated bread and wine, the atoms of those things become part of our bodies and Christ becomes one with our spirit."

"All right," Rose said. "What does that have to do with what just happened."

"What just happened was my memory of another conversation I overheard years ago in the parish hall. Someone had their knickers in a knot because they knew of someone who had not been baptized but had received communion. Nor had they been turned away from continuing to receive the bread and cup when the priest found out.

"'What would be the point?'" the old padre asked the kvetchers. 'We say we believe in the Real Presence of Christ in the bread and in the wine. So they had literally received Christ Jesus into themselves and we believe His spirit had become joined with theirs. Baptism seems a bit redundant, doesn't it?'

"'So Baptism doesn't matter then?' the complainers asked.

"'No, of course not,' he said. 'It matters a great deal if you want to join the church and vote and hold office. That's about membership, not the means of grace.'"

"So what does this have to do with what just happened?" Rose wanted to know.

"I just had another moment of clarity," I told her. "I realized that while I call myself an agnostic, I have, in fact, been a Christian all these years."

"So you think you might be going to hell for all your sins or something?"

"Quite the contrary. I just realized why I had the reaction I did to the crucifix. It was like waking up from amnesia and realizing who I was. Or, maybe, who I belonged to. What is unsettling is wondering how I could be so blind."

"So does this mean everything changes?" Rose asked quietly.

Seeing the look on her face I took her in my arms. She started to resist, then held me tight, almost clinging. "No, not for a moment," I told her. "It means there is a whole side of me I never knew was there."

"So where do we go from here?"

"I don't know but I suspect that will be apparent at some point. Maybe I need to talk to the padre."

"Just don't shut me out," Rose said. She sounded almost like a child begging. "Please."

"Not for a moment," I assured her. It was a promise I intended to keep, no matter what. I hope I did.

The parish priest was someone I had never met. I was aware the padre had moved on and that there had been an interim. The newspaper had dutifully reported the appointment of a new vicar. Somehow in the two or three years she had been in place our paths had not crossed. I had attended Christmas Eve services every year and I could recognize her on the street. Yet we had somehow never been introduced.

Even so, she knew who I was when I called. "Ah, the mysterious Ralph Williams," she said. Her voice was very calm and reassuring. "Also known as the famous Cody Grey Adams."

"More like infamous," I replied lightly. "I'm never going to live that down. To tell the truth, though, I can't say that I've tried."

"Who would want to?" she asked. "*Midlife Crazy* is a masterpiece. I particularly appreciated Father Felix. I wish there were more of us like him."

"Thank you. I do, too. I liked working with him. I'm afraid

I did the last Vicar a disservice, however. A lot of people wanted to know if he was the model for the character."

"I hear a lot of folk want know if they were the models for other characters in the book."

"When they ask, I used to tell them, 'Yes, in bits and pieces.' Then they wanted to know which pieces."

"Of course," the vicar replied. "I suspect the reality is that most of these folk would not believe they were not interesting enough to include as a character."

"Yes, well, I've been very careful not to say as much. It is a small community."

The vicar chuckled. "There is that. How may I help you today Doctor Williams? Or is it Mister Adams?"

I was pleased that she had done her homework. "Well, Reverend Mother, I prefer given names. Real names. Around here I'm Ralph, not Cody. Cody is for book shows and glitz occasions."

She chuckled. It had a deep throaty timbre, "It's a deal, Ralph. I go by Ali or Alice, both short for Allison. My parents were big fans of Arlo Guthrie and the Louisville Lip. How may I help you?"

"My bride and I would like to talk with you about blessing our civil union. Sooner would be better. We have done things kind of backward. At some point we would like to talk to you about becoming members, as well. And we will soon have a child to baptize."

"Well, you, yourself, are already on the rolls as a long time member. I did see, however, that you have never been confirmed. Is that something we should talk about?"

"Yes, as a matter of fact, but in person. I find it much harder to understand what a person is saying over the telephone. I feel lost without all those nonverbal clues. That's the real skinny as far as I'm concerned."

We set up a time for Rose and I to come in and I felt good about the conversation when we were done. Rose seemed a little nervous about it when I told her. "I can cancel if you'd rather," I replied. "I thought we had agreed to go ahead."

"It's OK," she told me, punctuating her words with a hug. "Things are just coming at me pretty fast right now. I'm not used to people calling me up to have tea or go shopping. I don't know how to do those things. My mother was a flower child and never taught me."

"Wasn't there an aunt or someone else to show you the *ropas*?" I asked. "I always thought women were born know how to shop."

Rose smiled. "I can see how you might think that, sweet man, particularly growing up in the South. The thing is, I didn't have anything like a normal childhood. I did have one safe uncle who did as much as he could, but he lived out of state. Shopping with him was visiting a hardware or sporting goods store. I know quite a bit about guns and hand tools but not much about girly things. Based on my childhood, most of what I learned involved drinking until you keel over."

"Come, on," I replied. "That's ridiculous. You dress very well and your outfits look great."

"Yes, that's because I have girl friends who love to buy for me. If you think about it, you haven't seen me in very many outfits. I have six and those cover every occasion. Most of the times it's jeans and tees or hippy chick blouses. I don't even know what to wear to visit the vicar. Most of my clothes have gotten to the point they don't fit."

"What about some of the women you've met here? Is there anyone you might feel comfortable asking?"

Rose shook her head. "Have you looked at how they dress around here?"

It was then I had an inspiration. My best friend on the

faculty used to say one should avoid such brain storms. That particular day I ignored his sage advice. "I do," I said and dialed a number. I was lucky when the vicar answered. "Ali?" I asked. "I have a favor to ask. Do you like to shop?"

Rose's eyes were big as saucers and she tried to wave me off. I ignored her. "Does a bear like honey?" Ali asked. "What's the catch?"

"Rose needs someone familiar with the local stores to help her find what she needs. Think of it like being the fashion guide on a shopping safari to bag a suitable wardrobe. You would be armed with an empty credit card that needs filling. Sound interesting?"

"Are you kidding?" she asked. "Put her on the line."

As I thought, it took less than a minute for the two women to become as thick as thieves. After she hung up Rose turned to me and from the way she picked her words I could tell she was both happy and torqued. "Ali seems like a very good person but I really don't like it when people do that to me, Ralph. May I ask why you did?"

I shrugged. "I didn't know it would offend you. It seemed like a good idea at the moment. She's an outsider here, too, and I've heard good things about her. She dresses well, too, from what little I've seen. It occurred to me she might be a good friend for you. When the two of you were talking it seemed like I was right. Or was I?"

"That's not the point," Rose told me. "You had no way of knowing it but El Jerko the First did that kind of thing to me all the time. It was one of the many ways he used to put me down."

I had no idea how to respond to that but whatever Rose saw in my face apparently assured her. "It's all right, lover. You didn't know. I'm afraid your bride still has a lot of baggage." I started to say something but she touched a gentle finger to my lips.

I kissed her hand and then her lips. "As I recall, I said for better or for worse," I murmured.

"Then maybe I need to remind you of the better," she replied with a knowing smile.

That was the beginning of a wonderful friendship and the three of us ended up doing a lot of different things together. We never did end up visiting the vicar in her office. Most of our inquirer's instruction took place over the remains of a good meal at our dining room table or in front of our fireplace. While open fireplaces these may or may not be energy efficient, nothing else fosters the same sense of intimacy. Nor have I experienced anything as erotic as lying skin to skin with my love on the well finished leather of our couch in front of our fire and watching her passion come to life like a summer storm.

There were times when Ali would bring along a date on our excursions to the Twin Cities, but it was mostly us three. After Richard was born on Christmas Day our trips were less frequent until he was old enough to travel and we could bring him along, too. Yet our outings were mostly us three and Rick seemed to enjoy brief sabbaticals from Mom and Dad. One of our neighbors had a son his age and the two of them became the best of friends.

Even so, Ali didn't date very often. As one might imagine, having a love life is almost impossible for a vicar in a small town in the Midwest. There were few eligible bachelors around who were not intimidated by Ali's striking physical stature. She was taller than most men and looked like a Valkyrie. There were even fewer men who were not intimidated by her intelligence and education, or the razor sharp edge of her wit.

Even so, it was the fact she was a vicar that put most men

off before they got to know the warm and delightful woman behind the collar. I hate to admit it but I was among those numb-nuts who so unjustly saw her in this light. So I had never bothered to get to know her when first she came to town and that, as my beloved put it so well, was my loss.

When my love said this, she was grinning. "On the other hand, it was my gain," she added. "And I'm very selfish when it comes to my Ralph. I want him all to myself." Then, of course, she had to show me.

It was on one of our excursions that the three of us encountered the Twin Cities Gospel Choir. It was a life changing event. I had wanted to see these folk for many years but Angela wouldn't go to their gospel celebrations with me. The reason was that not long after we first met we attended a gospel event at her father's church. It was our last. Angela said I was far too enthusiastic dancing around in the pews and waving my arms and clapping. She told me she found this mortifying.

My father-in-law smiled when I told him about this later. "I have to agree with my daughter on one point," he allowed. "You were really caught up in the Spirit." Then he chuckled. "People in the congregation talked about it for months. Nobody had ever seen a white man dance and sing quite like that before."

When I tried to apologize, the reverend shook his head and waved me off. "No, son, no need to apologize. All that's between you and the Lord. Just like praying. Never apologize for that."

Rose and Ali both thought this was funny when I told them about it on the way to the Cities. "I was right," my bride said. "You're a mystic. No wonder all that stuff happened in Cowtown."

Ali, of course, wanted to know exactly what stuff Rose

was talking about. "I think Ralph needs to tell you," Rose replied. "It's his story."

"Go ahead, sweetheart," I told her. "I've never heard your take on all of it."

"See why I love the lug so much?" Rose said to Ali and plunged into the story.

When Rose was done, Ali shook her head. "Wow! Talk about burning bush experiences! Do you have any idea how blessed you are, Ralph?"

"Of course, I do," I replied. "All I have to do is to look at my bride. She was the angel Someone sent to un-wedge my head and open my eyes."

Ali chuckled and Rose smiled. "I'll remind you of that the next time there's a serious wedging," she told me and I knew it was a promise.

"I'm serious, Ralph," Ali replied. "There are people who yearn for that kind of experience. With you they seem to happen left and right."

"Well, the people who yearn don't know what they're after," I assured her. "Not from where I stand. It's like living in the middle of a tornado, knowing you're completely out of control and totally helpless. It's terrifying."

Ali nodded. "I imagine it is, she replied. Then she sighed and spoke almost as if to herself. "Then there's the other issue, too."

"The other issue?" I asked.

"Yes. These things are gifts but they are not given only for the benefit of those chosen to receive them. The deeper question is what the Giver had in mind. Why were they given to you, Ralph? What purpose are they intended to serve?"

"I have absolutely no idea, assuming they were gifts and not something else."

"What else would they be?" Ali asked. I was certain she

knew exactly what I had not said.

"A burden," I told her. "There is nothing warm and fuzzy living inside them."

Ali nodded and smiled. "That's right," she told us and I knew she was speaking from experience. "There's a wonderful story about Theresa of Avila I like. Are you familiar with her?"

"Not really. Spanish mystic, fourteenth or fifteenth century. That's about it."

"Sixteenth century, actually. She was an ecstatic nun, like what's known today as a charismatic Christian. She was also very plain spoken and didn't hesitate to take God to task. The story is that she was crossing a stream riding on a donkey deep in prayer. The donkey stumbled and Theresa was left hanging upside down on the donkey with her head in the cold water. Getting to her feet she took God to task for allowing something bad to happen to someone who was a true friend to him. God supposedly answered that he chastised all his friends like that. To which Theresa replied, 'No wonder you have so few!'"

Rose and I both laughed. "I can relate to that," I told Ali. "So you think there's something or other I'm supposed to do. Any idea what that is?"

"Not at all," the madre told me. "All I can tell you is to be open and attentive. I may be wrong but I think everything that happened in Fort Worth was intended to get your attention. Sort of like a celestial tap on the shoulder. I think tonight was a reminder that you need to respond."

"Seems more like a kick in the ass," I offered.

"I imagine it does. The point is that I don't think you'll be at peace with yourself until you comply. At least, that was my experience with becoming a priest. It was hard to accept the idea I was called, but once I did, everything began to fall into place. The way it all came together was very odd, too. No way could I see a human being making things happen the way they did. There was too much coincidence."

Rose smiled. "And coincidence is God's way of being anonymous."

"Exactly," Ali replied. "Einstein was right on with that one."

We arrived at our destination about then so we left it at that. Yet I made myself a mental note to ask Ali about all this later. She was the first person I met who seemed to know what she was talking about. She later told me she was known as a "no bullshit priest" among her colleagues, and she seemed to be pleased to embrace it. "This means I will always be in trouble with the powers that be, but so what? So was the Boss and so was Elija."

"Just don't get yourself crucified," I told her. "We like having you around." Rose nodded.

Ali sighed. "I wish certain people in my flock felt that way. It seems impossible to win them over."

"Well, speaking *ex cathedra* for Father Felix, the only people you need to please are God and yourself. A lot or people set themselves up so that there is no pleasing them. Not even God can."

Ali laughed. "I didn't realize Father Felix had a *cathedra* from which to speak."

"She sounds like an English major," Rose observed.

"I think you're right about setting themselves up," Ali continued. "They seem to prefer living life in a constant uproar and insist on impossible expectations."

"Or maybe they are just addicted to drama," Rose said softly. "My family growing up sure was. I imagine they still are. I haven't spoken to them in years." There were tears in her eyes after she spoke. "I'm sorry. That's a real downer. Let's talk about something else."

Ali leaned over the passenger's seat and hugged Rose. "Of course, we can, Rose. What would you like to talk about? Or we can be quiet, too."

Rose was silent for a long moment. Then she turned to me and smiled. "How 'bout them Vikings!" It was so unexpected I almost drove off the road laughing.

The gospel event that evening was a workshop, not a concert, which made things even better. The director was a small man with a mighty voice and when he opened his mouth to sing it looked like he was about to swallow a cantaloupe. The sound he produced was incredible and he invited us to sing responsively. So he sang what he wanted us to repeat, and he stopped to teach us things like how to project our voices using our diaphragm.

The wonderful thing was that as we sang we gained confidence and within a half hour he had us belting out Amazing Grace and Joyful, Joyful We Adore Thee. Once he had us singing from the heart, he taught us to sing with the body. Starting with the simple Amen chorus, he asked us to stand and clap in time and then he moved on to our feet. The objective was to get us to worship with our entire bodies and I found it amazing to see the nave filled with staid Norwegians clapping their hands, swaying in the pews, and singing their hearts out when he returned us to Hymn to Joy.

I turned to my beloved and held out my hand for her to join me when the music began. Her eyes were wide with fright as she shook her head. Then Ali caught my eye, grinning and when I looked at Rose again, she nodded.

Since were seated at the end of the pew it was easy for us to move into the center aisle and Ali and I began to dance and wave our arms as we clapped and sang. A moment later another couple joined us, and then another and another. The music director saw this and signaled to the pianist to keep the music going and he played the hymn all the way through again.

As I danced I felt a rush of energy I had not felt in more then forty years and as I turned, my eyes met Ali's. The connection between us was immediate and intense and I saw her start to pull back. Then some strange thing happened I cannot explain. It was like barriers going down as we held our gaze, one by one until we were completely open to one another. I had never been so vulnerable to another human being or known anyone more intimately, not even Rose. I wondered how this could be but the thought drifted off into the vast space around us like a balloon on the wind.

Then the music stopped and everyone applauded. We sat down and Ali said, "Wow! That was better than sex!"

Unfortunately, the director had raised his hands a moment before she spoke and there was one of those sudden silences that can happen in a noisy crowd. Ali had been speaking loud enough to be heard over the crowd and in the quiet church there was no one that could not hear every word she said.

The congregation was so shocked the silence seemed to go on forever. Ali's face turned bright red. Then someone tittered and the crowd roared with laughter.

It was the music director who came to Ali's rescue. "Well, praise the Lord!" he declared. "We'll count that as a blessing." The congregation laughed again and the director moved us on to something else. When the event was done, Ali beat a hasty retreat to the car. Rose and I took our time and I was aware of the odd looks we got. So was Rose and she kept her attention focused straight ahead.

I looked at my watch when we got to the car and I was

surprised to see we had been there for almost three hours. "Does anybody want to stop for dessert?" I asked, suggesting an IHOP we had seen on the way into town. Yet neither of the women answered and I headed for home.

After an hour of silence I had enough. I stopped at a family restaurant and said, "I need to get a cup of coffee. Anyone care to join me?"

Both of my companions were silent. "All right," I added. "I'll get it to go. You two might want to make a pit stop. It's still a long way home." Rose nodded and got out and a moment later, so did Ali.

When I came out of the washroom I saw my two passengers sitting in a booth at the very back of the restaurant. No one else was sitting anywhere nearby and if there was any other conversation, it was masked by the background music softly playing. It was elevator music, mostly easy-listening jazz and a waitress took our order. I could tell she was aware something was going on between Ali and Rose and she left us alone until the food came.

"I'm sorry, Rose," Ali began as I sat down but my bride shook her head. "I'm not upset with either of you," she told us. "I'm just upset. I feel like a bloated cow and watching you two dance just reminded me how fat and ugly I am right now. Then you both really connected and I really felt completely left out."

"Is it the connection that bothered you?" I asked her and Rose nodded. "How about you, Ali?" I asked.

"No, I think the director was right. I think it was a blessing, a gift from God. I wish I had what the two of you have."

"It really scared me," Rose said. "It felt like I was losing you, Ralph. It still does. I wish I could let myself go where you do."

"Sweetheart, you are my anchor. My touchstone to reality,

to sanity. I've been drifting since Angela died and I don't know why I'm having these experiences now. I wish I weren't but there doesn't seem to be much I can do about them. It's like getting a cold or hay fever. One moment I'm normal self and the next thing I know, I sneeze and I'm off in a whole new dimension. I wish I could just ignore these things. Or make them go away."

"I don't think you can, Ralph," Ali said. "I'm sorry if I'm butting into a private conversation, but I don't think Ralph would ever be happy ignoring them." She was looking at Rose as she said this.

Rose nodded and reached out and took Ali's hand. "I think you're right, Ali. At first what you two were doing really pissed me off. What it looked like from where I sat was that you two were having intense sex. You were totally connected."

Ali smiled. "Let me tell you something, Rose. If I thought I could find sex like that, I'd ditch the collar! What turned it around for you just now?"

"I remembered how well I know my man. I cannot imagine him doing something like that to hurt me."

"I can't, either," Ali said, nodding. They both looked at me like they were inspecting a cut of meat.

"Well, if I have a vote, I'll make it unanimous," I told them. "We really do need to talk about all this, and soon. But we've got a long ride home and I'm feeling my years."

"Oh," Rose said, perking up. "That means I can drive. I'm wide awake." Seeing the look on my face she laughed. "I'll be careful, grandpa, I promise."

"God help us!" I told Ali. "I hope you brought your Rosary."

Things changed among the three of us after that. We spent a lot of time doing things together that fall. It was our second year there and when winter came we spent a lot of time in front of the fireplace. Rick took to having Ali around very quickly after he arrived and adopted her as a second mother. Then one evening an unexpected blizzard blew in late in May and Ali stayed with us or four days and nights until it blew itself out. We were literally snowed in.

The second evening of the blizzard we were all in front of the fire sipping wine. Rick was asleep in Ali's lap in the recliner and Rose and I were wrapped up under a warm blanket on the leather couch. At some point Rick woke up needing a change. I started to get up and do it but Ali stopped me. "Let me do it," she said. Looking at Rick she added, "Smells like you need a fresh diaper. Do you want aunty Ali to clean you up?" She made clicking sounds with her tongue and he gurgled and laughed. "Why don't you pour us some more wine?" she said to me.

"I think those were the last two bottles," I called after her. It was hard for me to believe the three of us had polished off a magnum of Provence rosè.

"All fresh and clean," Ali said a few moments later. She gave Rick to us when she brought him back and started to sit down. Yet when she did, he fussed and reached out for Ali. So she came back and took him in her arms. He immediately calmed down.

Even so, Rick began to fuss again when Ali tried to sit down with him in the recliner and he reached out for Rose again. "Make up your mind, kiddo," Ali said as she got up and brought Rick back to us. Then, when she started to return to her chair, he fussed again.

"I think he wants both of you to hold him together," I said, getting up and taking my son. Once again Rick calmed down when I set him between the two women. Yet, when I tried to sit in the recliner, he fussed and reached out for me.

"I think he wants his whole family," Ali laughed. "Why

don't you sit between Rose and me?"

Sure enough, that was exactly what Rick wanted and he immediately fell asleep in my lap. "This is nice," Ali murmured. "That wine is wonderful, maybe a little too much."

"Yes, it is," Rose replied, turning and raising her lips to my cheek. Then she leaned across me and kissed Ali on the cheek, too. "One wonderful family," Rose added, looking into Ali's eyes. Then she kissed Ali again, full on the lips. "Thank you for being part of it."

"Rose...." Ali answered. Her pupils were dilated fully and in them I could see desire mixed with fear in them.

"Shhh," Rose whispered, kissing Ali again. This time she lingered and I felt her reach out to caress Ali, who moaned. "I've wanted to do that for a long time," Rose told her. She looked at me, uncertain.

Ali turned her eyes and looked into mine. "Go for it," I whispered and she gave me a kiss that left no doubt how she felt or what she wanted. Then she kissed Rose again, reaching out and grasped me in a tender place.

We all awoke in our huge bed the next morning. At first, we didn't speak except to wish one another a good morning. I crawled out from between the two women and slipped into the bathroom. The room was chilly and I looked around for a bathrobe and some house shoes. When I looked up Ali had crawled out of bed, bare as a bear and I watched her as she crossed the room to the bath. I was struck by how beautiful she was in the morning light.

I checked our son but he was still sound asleep and I didn't wake him. Let sleeping babies lie, I thought as I began to make a pot of coffee. Once done with that I began to prepare breakfast.

"He cooks breakfast, too?" I heard Ali ask. When I turned to answer, Rose was there beside her, smiling at me with her eyes. Just then Rick let us know he was awake and ready to rumble. Rose went to get him and I gave Ali a good morning kiss. I was struck by how sweet and gentle it was. "Thank you," she whispered softly and kissed me again.

I returned to my cooking, surprised I was not having a hangover. I was very grateful, too. On the other hand, the wine was not that strong, only about 12% alcohol by volume, and we had opened the first bottle long before supper. So over seven hours we had each consumed the equivalent of roughly one ounce of Everclear per hour. Our liver would process half of that leaving the other half to do its thing.

It was then my eye fell on the two bottles we had been drinking. One of them was empty but the other was still half full. So we had been drinking quite a bit less than I'd thought. About three quarters of an ounce I figured.

I found that both scary and reassuring. I found it reassuring that we had not fallen into bed because we were drunk. What was scary was that while the wine may have relaxed us and dulled our inhibitions, we were not drunk when it happened. To put it another way, we had each made the choice to do exactly what we did.

The odd thing was that I didn't feel jealous of Ali. Not that I would want to feel that. Jealousy is a slimy bottom feeder that can destroy what it desires. I find it quite uncomfortable, a vile, malicious spirit that needed to be exorcised. Then it crossed my mind that we at least had a priest on our side to do just that.

We were silent at breakfast, each of us lost in our own thoughts. After breakfast we all went about our business as best we could. Outside the blizzard still raged and the temperature hovered in the teens. Local forecasters on the only radio station we could get marveled at the ferocity of the storm and talked about famous blizzards that had pretty much shut down this part of the state for days on end. They kept predicting the storm would abate and issued dire warnings against trying to travel. Fortunately, the power stayed on and the telephone system still worked, as did the Internet. Ali called the wardens of her parish to let the congregation know she was all right, and that morning she made a number of other calls to check on those who were home-bound.

I made us a late lunch from a frozen dish of lasagna I found in the deep freeze. It had been in the freezer so long I wondered if it was still good. Once it was warm it was easy to cut off the freezer burnt edges and I was surprised to find it still quite good.

After lunch I suggested a long winter's nap. Ali thought that was a good idea. "Together?" she asked.

"You two go ahead," Rose said. "I think I'll stay up and keep Rick company when he wakes."

"Are you sure?" Ali asked. "It feels funny without you. I'll stay up, too."

"No," Rose said. "I guess we need to talk about this at some point but I don't want to ruin it."

"Me, too," Ali replied. "It was so beautiful. It wasn't just the fire and the wine and the storm, either. Something very beautiful happened."

Rose nodded. "Maybe we need to let our bodies do the talking for now. We'll know when it's time to talk."

"I don't want to stop in the mean time," Ali said. "If what we've had is all we get, I'm very grateful. But I don't want it to stop."

"Neither do I," my bride said, then turned to me and asked, "How about you, Ralph?"

"Are you kidding? With the two most beautiful women in the world in my bed? I think it was a gift to all of us. I definitely want to go on but it has to be what we all want."

"Yes, I think it was a gift, too, but what are we supposed to do with it?" I took Rose in my arms and a moment later Ali embraced us both.

"Well, one thing we can do is celebrate it!" Ali said. "I think that would be a good start."

Rose nodded. "Yes. You two go ahead and I'll join you later if I can."

Making love to Ali alone seemed strange at first. I suggested that we cuddle for a while first to get over the awkward feeling and Ali thought that was good. So we began to undress each other gently, working our way down. The last items were her socks and shoes and as I removed them she put her hands on my head. As I laid aside her last sock she pulled me close and I kissed her. "God, Ralph!" she declared. "I don't think I can wait." So I kissed her again, deeply, and heard her cry out over and over as shudder after shudder racked her beautiful frame.

Afterwards as we lay quietly entwined I drifted off to sleep. I was awakened by the sound of Ali weeping. When I looked to see what was wrong, Rose was there, holding Ali as she wept. I joined her as we cradled Ali between us.

When the tempest had passed Ali kissed each of us. I started to ask what was wrong, but that seemed rather obvious. "I had the most awful dream," Ali told us. "I was naked and in chains, and very pregnant, and every other priest in the diocese was there, too. We were in the cathedral and I was being deposed. You two were there, too, but you were naked and in chains, too. The Devil was there and his job was to flog me after I had been thrown out into the street. So was the chief apostle of the Mormon Church but I don't know why he was there. And everyone but you two was laughing."

"Dear God!" Rose declared. "How awful!"

"Why were you being thrown out?" I asked. "Was it because of us?"

Ali nodded and started to cry again. "I dreamed that somebody found out what we were doing and called the Archdeacon. He's the bishop's hatchet man."

Rose and I looked at each other. We were both at a loss for words. "How can anything so beautiful be wrong?" Ali asked.

"It isn't wrong," I asserted and Rose nodded. "Not for us and I don't think for you, either. Just because other people may think it's wrong doesn't mean that they are right. I think we probably need to talk."

"Isn't that what we're doing?" Rose asked.

"Yes, but the fireplace is in the living room," I told her, jumping up and standing on the bed. I had no idea how I got so angry so fast. "That doesn't make a bit of sense, does it?" I growled. "I need to pace. I want to kick ass and take names!"

Ali looked at me in disbelief and started laughing. Rose tried to keep a straight face but started giggling, too. "What in the hell are you laughing about?" I demanded, indignant.

"You," Rose answered. "I wish you could see yourself right now. Don Quixote, charging into battle naked as a jaybird."

Suddenly the absurdity of my response became clear to me and my anger left as quickly as it had come. "I need caffeine," I told them, pulling on my pants and shirt. Who wants some hot chocolate?"

Rose and Ali looked at one another. "Who is this strange man?" Rose asked.

Once I had the fire going we all sat down around it sipping cocoa. Rick was up, too, lying snuggled in his bassinet, cooing to himself as he played with a string of wooden beads. I was staring into the fire and I became aware both women were waiting for me.

"A penny for your thoughts, Ralph," Rose asked and Ali nodded.

"I was just thinking about where to begin," I said. "I think it would be most helpful to start at the bottom line and work our way up. What's the most important thing in your life, Ali?"

"That's an easy one. God."

"Why don't you invite God into this?" I asked. "Are you all right with that, Rose?" She looked scared but she nodded and Ali said a wonderful short prayer. Later I found out the first part was written by an American theologian named Reinhold Niebuhr and is commonly known as the Serenity Prayer. Yet Ali added her own words to it, asking grace to live our lives a day at a time and to celebrate every moment. I found it quite moving and I saw Rose nodding when Ali was done.

"All right," I continued. "Next to God, what is the most important thing in your life."

"Up to yesterday, I would have said being a priest."

"And today?"

"That's just it. I don't know any more. You guys are all right up there at the top of the list. That includes Rick, too."

"Us or having a family?" I asked, gently as I could.

"You know how to cut through the bullshit, don't you, Ralph?" There was an edge to her voice I had never heard before. "You three is who I said and who I meant."

"I wasn't challenging you, Ali. I was clarifying. I guess we need to assess what we are. Rose?"

"We are a family, Ralph. That's the most important thing in my life. I would like Ali to be part of our family. I don't know how that can be but that's what I want? How about you?"

"You and Rick are the most important things in my life,

Rose. You have to come first, before me or anyone else. I think it would be a wonderful thing having Ali as a partner with us if we can work it out. What do you think, Ali?"

"I'm scared, Ralph. You guys have a wonderful thing. I don't want to mess it up."

I turned to Rose. "I think she dodged the question." She nodded.

I turned back to Ali. "The question is what does Ali want?"

"I would like to be part of your family, too," she said with tears in her eyes. "But what happens if it doesn't work out?"

"Rose and I are in for better or for worse and I knew that was what I wanted from the start," I answered. "It turned out that she needed some time to get her mind around it and I gave her as much time as she needed." I looked at Rose, who nodded and I went on. "This is much different and probably more difficult. No, let's say more challenging. We all know that."

Rose broke in. "So is it all right with you to give her time to figure it out for herself? I think we should."

"I agree, just like we did for you. We need to give her as much time as she needs. Is that all right with you, Ali? We'll have to work out details and issues as we go but will you have us?"

"God, yes!" Ali cried, bursting into tears. Rose and I moved close and held her until the weeping stopped. "So what do we need to decide first?" Ali asked.

Rose and I looked at one another but neither of us spoke. It was Rick who answered the question by crying to let us know he had filled his diaper.

8

Turning Points

It didn't take Ali long to come to a decision. She told us later that her decision had been made by the time the blizzard had blown itself out that week. Yet she waited for a couple more weeks to let us know.

During that time, Ali was with us every minute she had free. Yet, she also had to be very careful to spend enough nights at her tiny apartment, to keep up appearances. Even so, when she needed to stay away, she called us every morning to tell us she loved us, and every evening to say good night. Sometimes she would drive out to join us for lunch.

It was on a Sunday evening that Ali told us she was sure she wanted to be our partner. She also wanted to spend a lot more time with us. "We need to be part of each other's daily lives," is how she put it. "I don't know how to do that and stay on at the church, too. And if I just move in, the gossips will have a feeding frenzy. Maybe I just need to resign."

"Not necessarily," I told her. "It depends on how we do it. Didn't you tell us you wanted to find a bigger place? If I remember right, you told us that way back before the night we went to the Cities. Aren't people in the parish aware of that?"

"Oh, yes. A couple of women from the altar guild have been helping me look for a bigger place, one I can afford. We thought something might come open after Christmas but nothing has. At least, nothing I would care to rent."

"Well, couldn't we rent you our basement?" I asked, looking at Rose, who smiled and nodded. "Do you think a dollar a month is too much?"

Ali smiled. "I thought about asking if we could do that, Ralph, but it's got to look real."

"That's simple enough. We can draw up a contract. Then give us a check each month for whatever you're paying now and we'll put it into a household account we can all draw from. You can keep the bank account you have now to manage appearances and deposit your paycheck there." I looked at Rose again and she nodded.

"It seems too simple," Ali told us.

"It doesn't have to be," Rose told her. "We can make it as simple or as complicated as we like." She grinned. "You can use the master bedroom in the basement for your dressing room and put your makeup out in the bathroom. Is that complicated enough?"

"Will you all come and visit me down there?" Ali asked, smiling.

"When is your lease up?" I asked.

"That's not a problem," Ali replied. "I've been there long enough that it's month-to-month now."

"Good. Give them notice tomorrow and I'll hire a couple of guys I know to move your stuff. When do you want to move?"

"You don't have to hire anyone," Ali told me. "All I have are my clothes and some books and personal stuff. I rented it furnished so I don't have to worry about furniture. I can move everything else myself a little at a time."

"Ali," Rose said gently but in a tone that left no room for no argument, "You are becoming part of this family. You don't have to do things on your own and you need to let us help. I will help you pack and we can let Ralph's guys do the carrying. They can use the money. Especially at this time of year."

I nodded. "These are the same guys who do the yard work and keep our driveway cleared when it snows. They know to keep their mouths shut."

Ali looked at us. Then the tears started and Rose and I held her close. "You have us," Rose told her. "You never have to be alone again. We're your family now. For better or for worse."

As careful as we were to keep our new union to ourselves, Ali's move to our place did not go unnoticed. She was very careful to let the altar guild ladies know that she had found a much larger place and where it was. As a result, the details of our earlier friendship became grist for the gossip mongers. As a good friend told me one day in the Post Office, a lot was said in significant looks and raised eyebrows. We were in line as we talked and I noticed a few folk who seemed to be tracking every word.

"Yeah," I told my friend. "It worked out well for all of us. She wanted a bigger place and Rose can use the help looking after Rick. We've got plenty of room."

So Ali's becoming our tenant was talked about most thoroughly. Not that any of this was anyone's business but ours, but such is the nature of small-town America. I am told that life in small towns is painfully boring and gossip is the most popular local sport. I wouldn't know. As a writer I am off in my own little world half the time, anyway. I may listen to gossip from time to time but it stops with me. I do not pass it on.

One of the things the busybodies disliked the most was how much privacy the new arrangement gave Ali. As the most eligible professional woman in town, her activities had been closely monitored since the day she arrived. They were a favorite source for our Olympic carriers of tales. Of course, none of what they said had to be true. When facts were few, the chin-wag weavers made them up *ex nihilo*.

This had a number of consequences and few of these were beneficial. Others turned out well, despite the malice of the tittle-tattles. One of the more odious incidents was when an ambitious soul from the tax assessor's office showed up at our door one day wanting to inspect the place. He was rather ruffled when Rose made him wait on the stoop while she fetched me. Nor was I in any mood to invite him in or tolerate any other foolishness.

"Why are you here?" I asked quite bluntly. "I've lived here for thirty years, more or less, and this is the first visit I've had from anyone in your office."

"Well, I understand you're turning your home into a duplex," the told me. "That will affect your tax status, of course."

"Where do you get your information?" I asked. "For the record, it's incorrect."

"That's for you to prove to me," he replied.

"Horse hockey!" I declared. "I don't have to prove anything. The burden of proof is on you. That's the law. Where's your probable cause? What's your source of information?"

"Well, it's pretty well known all over town," he told me. "Are you denying it?"

I ignored his question. "Are you telling me that your source of information is public gossip? God help us, man! Don't you understand how that can come around and bite you?"

The odious little fellow just glared at me. I could see he had no sense of what I was telling him. "What if someone started a nasty rumor about you?"

"Well, I haven't done anything to start rumors," he asserted primly.

"Do you really think that matters? People make up slander all the time."

Then I had another thought. "I just realized I don't know you from Adam," I told him. "How do I know you're who you say you are? Do you even have any kind of credentials?"

"There!" he declared, handing me a business card. It did reveal that someone from the tax office was an appraiser but there was no picture on the card.

I pointed this out to the man and invited him to leave. He balked at this and I reminded him that he was trespassing. "You show up here without credentials and without a warrant, having come here allegedly to inspect our home. Your allegations are based on local gossip which you have not apparently tried to verify, and now you refuse to leave. What do you think my lawyer is going to do with that? Now get out of here!"

I stepped back in the house and locked the door. The next thing I did was to call the county sheriff and lodge a complaint. He's a good friend, one I have actively supported in every election, and when I told him what happened, he laughed. "Yeah, Gus," the sheriff said. "He thinks he's Elliot Ness. You're not the first one to call. He does have the right to come on your property to assess it, but he needs to identify himself. Did he do that?"

"All he showed us was a business card. Doesn't he have any official ID?"

"Yes, and he's supposed to show it, but he doesn't always remember to carry it." The sheriff paused. I could almost see him come to a decision. "Just between us and the gatepost, Doctor Williams, I think Gus enjoys pushing people around. I expect I'll be hearing from him next." There was a world of meaning in the way he sighed.

"Well, I hope I haven't made your job more difficult, Sheriff. I'm not asking you to do anything except note my official complaint in your work journal. Mostly, I want you to be aware of the situation in case he makes a stink or does something foolish. I would have been happy to let him see the place if he hadn't come on like gangbusters."

"Like I said, you're not the first who's come to me about Gus, Doctor Williams." His tone was not quite as warm as before. "I'm afraid you won't be the last and I am making a note of it in my work journal right this minute."

The sheriff paused and I waited. "The thing is, Doctor, our county tax assessor will be stepping down due to illness and Gus is the senior guy in the office. He's also the only one who's filed for the special election to fill his boss' place. I hate to say it, but it may get worse before it gets better." He paused, then added, "Unless, of course, some other upright citizen files or gets drafted and wins." When he said this I could hear he was clearly amused. "You know, of course, you could file if you wanted to. I'd be willing to bet you could win, too."

I laughed. "Oh, no, you don't, Mike. I saw you palm that ace. Besides, I feel sure someone else will file. I'm surprised no one has."

"You haven't seen their pay scale, but there's something else. There are also those who claim there is a curse on the position. Not one of the last three tax assessors has died of old age. Two were shot and killed, as a matter of fact. The other died in a car crash. There are some mean yahoos living back in the woods around here. I never go out on a call alone any more and neither will my deputies."

"Why are these people so touchy?" I asked.

"In a word, meth," he replied. "People don't realize it but this county is right up near the top of the list for production of methamphetamine in the state. We've got too many abandoned farm houses and making the stuff is not that hard. They can move in, produce for a week or two, and move on to another abandoned place. We simply don't have the resources to do much more than give them a hard time."

I thanked the sheriff for his time and for his effort in the drug wars on our behalf. Then I poured myself a fresh cup of coffee and sat down in front of the picture window. I sat there a long time looking at the lake and thinking about what I'd learned.

As I was sitting, there I remembered something I used to drill into my students. It was something Edmund Burke once said about the triumph of evil. All it takes for those of evil will to win is for good people to do nothing. Nazi Germany is the best example I know, but South Africa and the deep South come close.

I sat there until Rose walked in after a while and joined me, carrying our son. Seeing me, of course, Rick demanded to sit in my lap. I was in the middle of telling Rose what the sheriff had said when Ali showed up for lunch. When she did, Rick abandoned me in a flash and reached out for her.

When she heard what had happened, Ali was quite disturbed. "That stupid little toad!" she declared. "How dare he!" Then she looked at us sadly. "I am so sorry. I had no idea something like this could happened. Maybe this wasn't such a good idea, me living here." It was clear her heart was breaking when she said this.

"Horse shit!" Rose declared. The way she said it shocked both of us. I have never heard her speak with more force. "This is your home, Ali, and we are your family. I'm not about to let that little chicken shit-bag ruin it for us."

"Chit-baa!" Rick declared in the same tone of voice and every bit as forceful. He was delighted to have a new word to exercise. "Chit-baa! Chit-baa! Chit-baa! Chit-baa!" Despite the situation, we couldn't help laughing. Naturally, this delighted Rick and I could almost see his little brain filing it away for later. Then he tried the other new word he had just learned to see what effect it had. "Hose-chit! Hose-chit! Chit-baa! Hose-chit! Chit-baa!" Nor could we all help laughing again.

"Oh, dear," Rose said. She sighed, smiling. "We've created a monster." Then she grew serious. "What are we going to do, Ralph?"

"I think the first thing is to talk to the lawyer. I don't think we have enough for a restraining order, but if we do I'll have him file for it." Then I grinned. "The sheriff suggested I run for Tax Assessor. The current one will be retiring because of poor health and Mister Hose-chit is the only one who has filed."

"You're not seriously considering it, are you?" Rose asked. She looked worried.

"Of course, not," I replied. "That's the last thing I need. The only reason I'd file is if no one else does. Gus is bad enough as an assistant. Heaven help us if he gets himself elected boss."

I looked at Ali who was looking at us gravely. "What do you think, lover? You're awfully quiet."

I was surprised when Ali laughed. "I think it might be fun, to tell the truth. I think we could bury Gus under his own shit. Then you could fire him."

"I could fire him? You're assuming I would be the candidate. What about you or Rose?"

"Ali and I are newcomers around here," Rose replied. "You, on the other hand, are a famous writer who's lived here over thirty years. How well connected is old Hose-chit? It sounds like he may have torqued off a lot of other people, too."

"Turk!" Robbie declared. "Hose-chit turk!"

Ali laughed. "Hey, there's a good slogan: Turkeys are for Thanksgiving, not for public office."

"How about this? 'Dis-GUS-ted? Torqued by the Turk? Ralph will respect you.'"

"Hey!" I declared. "We're getting a bit ahead of ourselves here. I haven't decided to run, yet."

Both women looked at me like I was crazy. At that point I realized I was lost. Then I laughed. "You're right about that, Ali. It might be fun. Let's see if I can still file, first."

That was the beginning of my political career. Nor was it something I had ever imagined myself doing. Yet looking back, I cannot see what other real choice I had. Someone needed to do something, but no one else had. For good or ill, I was the one who had been drafted. It seemed like the best choice I had was to stop Gus before he ever got started.

So I filed for office. Nor did I stop there. I also worked hard to win. As FDR may or may not have put it, the first duty of any patriot is to get himself elected. Nor was there much point in filing without carrying through with a vigorous campaign.

As it turned out, the filing deadline was at the end of that week. I had planned to simply go to the right office to file and then put an ad in the local paper that I had done so. Yet neither Rose nor Ali thought this was a good idea. "No, Ralph, if you are going to do this, do it right," Rose told me. "What is the first thing politicians do when they decide to run for office?"

"I'm not a politician," I answered. "I don't intend to become one, either. So how would I know?"

Rose and Ali looked at one another. "He can be a bit dense, can't he?" Ali observed.

"I'd say a downright dumb-shit," Rose agreed. They both looked at me, grinning. "Think about it a moment," Rose told me. "What have you observed when politicians file for office?"

"I don't know what you're after," I told them. "They let the world know?"

"Yes, and how do they do that, by word-of-mouth?" Ali added. "Don't think local, Ralph. Think state and national."

"I won't be running at state and national levels," I complained. "That's how word gets out at a local level, by word-of-mouth. I guess I could go down to the local paper and take out an ad."

"No, you need to invite them to come to you," Rose said. "Hold a press conference. Invite the newspapers and the radio and television stations. Put it out on Facebook, too. You have an account, don't you?"

"I don't know. I used to."

"I'll take care of social media." Ali said.

Rose nodded. "I'll do papers, radio, and television. Where do you think it should be?"

"On the courthouse steps the day I file," I butted in. "Where else?"

The ladies looked at each other. "He seems to be catching on," Ali observed, and they both laughed.

"Now, what are you going to say?" Rose prompted.

That was the way my political career began, as an accident. The way it turned out, the sheriff was right. Gus was the only other candidate who filed. He didn't even get wind of my press conference until he saw it on the ten o'clock news that night. Unfortunately, the first person he thought to call was me but I knew how to record the call on our old answering machine. It used a small cassette and I was able to get every second of Gus' eleven-minute diatribe, earthy language and all.

When Gus finally ran down, I asked if that was all he had to say and he started all over again. "Gus!" I said in what Angie used to call my General's voice and he shut up. "You're repeating yourself. I got the drift the first two times around. Now if you don't have anything new to say, I'm going to hang up. Thanks for calling." He was squealing furiously when I rang off.

"I think he's pissed," Rose said dryly, grinning.

"What are you going to do with the tape?" Ali wanted to know. She looked concerned.

"Probably nothing," I said. "Unless Gus gets really nasty. Or attacks my family. Then it's no holds barred. I don't think it will come to that."

Rose and Ali looked doubtful but left it at that. As it turned out, I was wrong. Thank God because I have very low tolerance when my family is threatened. I don't like myself much when I let the dragon out to avenge, either.

The news conference itself was easy. Despite the short notice word had gotten around and there were a lot of townsfolk who attended. This I had not expected and I was nervous at first. Even so, I was told I didn't show it. Nor did it hurt that the first question out the chute was one Ali and Rose had planted with the local newspaper reporter. When I asked for questions the hands went up and I pointed to her and I had been instructed.

"Thank you, Doctor Williams," she said. "You have a long and distinguished career as a teacher. Why are you running for office now?"

"Thank you for asking, Marilyn. It's very simple. I don't like the way the tax people treat us. The tax people seem to think they can ride over us rough-shod. That's true of both the IRS and our state Department of Revenue. They think they can treat us like vermin and this tells me they do not understand the fact that they are public servants. They are supposed to serve us.

"I am sad to say the same is true of our county tax

department these days. I'm not talking about Arnold Sahlberg, either. Arnold is a good man and he has served us well. He has always been courteous to me and treated me fairly. I wish he was not retiring. I wish he didn't have to but he doesn't have much choice and neither do we.

"No, who I am talking about is my opponent. He is getting too big for his britches in my opinion. He is in charge of the office now, by default. He seems to think he can treat us taxpayers any way he wants and get away with it. What he does, his misbehavior, tells me that he does not respect us tax payers.

"I want to change that. I believe you want the same thing I do, fairness under the law and basic human respect. I don't want his contempt. I don't want his poor manners. I think it's time we taught him that we don't like bullies. We don't like politicians who forget they are public servants."

I was surprised how wound up I was getting. Yet, what I was doing felt right and I pointed to the local television station reporter. Like Marilyn, he was one of my former students.

"Thank you, Doctor Williams," he said. "What skills would you bring to the office."

I smiled. Ali told me to expect this question. "I can think of three right off the top of my head. One is that I always pay my bills on time. You can ask any merchant in town. Another is that I can balance my checkbook." This brought a chuckle from the crowd. "A third is that I am a good neighbor and have been for over thirty years. I am committed to the well being of this community and this county."

I paused, then added. "I also know my limitations. So if I find myself out of my depth, I know enough to ask for help."

I pointed to a second television news reporter, one who I did not know. "Thank you," he said. "Politicians are always making promises. What do you have to offer that your opponent cannot?"

"First of all, I am not a professional politician. So I won't promise you nickel beer and a chicken in every pot. But I can promise you some very simple things.

"First, I will put up a note on my shaving mirror. It will say, 'You are there to serve them.'" Someone in the back of the crowd clapped and whistled. I waved at them and said, "He charged me a dime to do that!" Several people laughed and the clapper whistled again.

I held up two fingers. "Second, I will put another sign up in our county tax office that says, 'Our public policy here is respect and fairness for every person we serve.'"

I held up a third finger. "Third, I will not draw my salary for personal use. It will be put into a special account open to your inspection. It will be used as I see fit to hire more help and to train the people we have. You deserve the best public service we can provide."

There was applause at this and I was about to end the conference when someone shouted from the back. "Who is Cody Adams?"

"I write mysteries, westerns, and love stories. Cody Grey Adams is my pen name and is also my registered trademark. So far I have written about thirty novels, all of them still in print. None of them have anything to do with politics. I think that's enough for now."

The questioner tried to shout another question but the small brass band of teens Ali had put together heard their cue and broke out loudly with "Stars and Stripes Forever." I was just as glad and moved around the crowd shaking hands. When we were done and headed home I felt like I had run a six-mile race.

"Damn, I'm glad I'm not a professional politician," I said

to my family.

"You're not half as glad as we are," Rose assured me and Ali nodded.

"You do understand, I hope, that this is a one-shot deal, don't you?" I continued. "It's only for a partial term. It's eighteen months until the general election and that gives me time to turn things around. After that I can step down. I can be the first Tax Collector in forty years who fails to die in office." Rose gave me a troubled look when I said this and Ali reached out to take her hand.

I was up early the next morning when I got a phone call. It was from Arnold Sahlberg and I was surprised to hear from him. After thanking me for my kind words, he got right to the point. "I really appreciate your stepping up to the plate," he told me. "I didn't realize how bad things were. Gus has always been good when I gave him good directions, so I made some phone calls to people I trust. Turns out they've been protecting me from what's been going on. Not much I can do about it now, of course, but you have my full support. Just so it's clear what I am saying, you have my full endorsement. I'll call the people I talked to, to put out the word."

"I don't know what to say, Mister Sahlberg." I said. "Thank you."

"You've earned it, Ralph," he chuckled. Yet, I could hear the pain in his voice. "Call me Arnold. Let's see if you're still thanking me after a month into the job. Your second term should be easier."

"I'm a one term guy," I replied. "I'm afraid there won't be a second one."

Arnold broke out laughing, but I could tell it cost him a lot of pain. "That's what they all say, me included. I'm grateful I had a chance to break the curse. You know what I'm talking about, Ralph?"

"You mean about the last three tax collectors dying in office?"

"Exactly. It will be a great relief to me when you're sworn in. I'm sorry for any mess I've left you."

"I'm sure it's not your doing," I replied. "You didn't choose to get sick."

"That's for damned sure!" He said, then chuckled drily. "On the other hand, you might say I did, given some of the poor choices I made along the way. You, I hear, are considered as something of a Puritan. Except for some of the books you write. Those are a little racy."

"A little racy?" I asked, feigning indignation. "I was shooting for downright naughty."

Arnold chuckled again. "I was being polite. Between us chickens, you're right and I think it's good writing. According to your opponent they're downright filth. You realize he's going to try to demonize you for them, don't you?"

"My answer is that people don't have to read them. I make no bones about them being for an adult reader. I never did, either. They're love stories and love is often pretty earthy."

"Well, I like them. The funny thing is that I would never have read them if I hadn't heard Gus pissing and moaning about how awful they were."

"Great. Maybe he will generate more local sales."

Arnold started to laugh but choked and ended up coughing, hard. "I think I better let you go," I said. "I appreciate your call. More than you know."

"Well, I appreciate what you're doing," he gasped. "Why don't you come by and have a cup of coffee when you get a minute? Don't worry about calling ahead, neither."

I thanked Arnold for his call and sat there for a while thinking about it. When I mentioned it to Ali over lunch, she nodded. "He's a good man. Don't put off getting by to see him. He's in pretty bad shape." I started to ask what she meant but Ali held up a hand and shook her head. "I really can't say much more than that, Ralph. He's one of my people."

"I didn't know he was a member of the parish."

"He's not on the official membership roll. On the other hand, the Church of England tends to consider everyone living in a legally defined area as being under its pastoral care. So my cure is everyone in this area."

"No wonder you're so busy," I said. "I hope you'll put in a good word for me. With Arnold," I clarified.

"I will if anyone asks," she said, smiling sweetly. "I can honestly tell them you're my landlord and a real sweetheart." Then she stretched and gave me a look I had come to know well. "You know, Rose and Rick won't be back until suppertime. We have the house to ourselves. Do you really want to talk politics right now?"

I awoke a good while later, still in bed. The light coming in the windows told me I had slept much longer than I intended. As I watched it fade, I thought about how lucky man I was to have two such beautiful women in my life when the door opened. Rose smiled in at me. "We were beginning to wonder if you were all right," she said, slipping out of her clothes and sliding under the covers. The sight of her in the buff never fails to move me. "Oh, my," she added a moment later. "We better do something about that."

There's not a lot to say about the campaign that year. Gus got wind of my health problems in Cowtown and tried to use it against me. That backfired when my long time physician let it be known I was fit as a fiddle, as he put it in his report. "Seventy is the new fifty and in his shape he could see a hundred."

Not satisfied with that, Gus tried to attack my little family but that backfired. Television cameras were very kind to Rose, as were the reporters, and most of the photos published showed her by my side carrying Rick. Our little man, of course, thought all the hoopala was great fun and rarely cried when others were around.

Since we live in a fairly small county, I was able to cover most of the rural areas in the six weeks after filing. Ali knew someone who had worked for the last federal census and he was able to suggest some things that saved us a lot of back-tracking. Later, when I talked to the sheriff, I learned our census friend had also helped us avoid most of the trouble spots where meth was produced. I was very concerned about missing a big part of our constituency until Ali pointed out two things. One was that meth dealers don't vote and, two, they are not tax payers. Like moonshiners in another era, they have also been known to take a pot-shot at the revenuers.

The people I was able to visit in the outlying areas of the county were hospitable and seemed pleased that I had taken the trouble to seek them out. They seemed open to what I had to say, as well. I was surprised how many of them had their own stories of encounters with Gus, mostly in the six months Arnold Sahlberg had been on medical leave.

This came up when I dropped in to see Arnold four weeks into the campaign. His wife met me at the door and I was shocked to see how bad he looked. He had lost a great deal of weight and his sickly gray skin hung loosely on what had once been a large frame.

I tried to hide my shock but Arnold was still sharp. "Looks like hell, doesn't it?" he asked. "The thing is, it's worse than it looks." He grinned, trying to make a joke and failing miserably.

I was having trouble finding my voice. Seeing him lying in

bed like that brought back those awful last days with Angie. I could barely see through the tears in my eyes and Arnold nodded.

"Oh, that's right," he said. Your wife died of cancer, didn't she? I'm sorry to remind you of that. My wife is having a hell of a time." He waved me into a rocking chair next to the bed where he lay.

"I appreciate your coming by," he told me. "Believe it or not, I'm having a good day and I'm damned grateful for it. Tell me what's going on with the campaign. I hear good things about you."

I told him what we had been doing in the rural areas, alternating visits there with those in town. Early on there had been a meet-the-candidates event put on by a local concerned voter's alliance and I had spoken to various civic groups, as well. "One advantage is that I can campaign in the daytime when Gus has to work."

"Who says Gus is actually working?" Arnold asked. "The girls in the office tell me he's never there and doesn't do a thing when he is. My wife has seen him out and about around town when he should have been at the office. He is the supervisor now."

"Maybe he's using personal leave time," I suggested. "I think me filing really scared him."

Arnold shook his head sadly. "This was a long time before you filed. I never would have thought it of him. He sure had me fooled."

I sensed that Arnold wanted to tell me more but I didn't know how to ask. He smiled. "You're a good, honorable man, Ralph."

I chuckled. "It takes one to know one, Arnold."

Arnold started to laugh but ended up gasping for air. I got up to do what I could to help but he waved me back to my chair. "Don't make me laugh, Ralph. It really hurts when I do. One more thing this damned disease has taken."

Arnold's face turned grave. "It hurts to say it but I have come to believe Gus is one of the most dishonest man I have ever seen. Up to now he's kept it well hidden, and if I could fire his ass, I would. Believe you me. The first thing I would suggest you do is bring in an outside auditor. Put Gus on paid leave and do it immediately."

"That's assuming I win."

"My sources tell me you will, and by a landslide, too. So you need to hit the ground running."

I nodded, but I was very uncomfortable with the direction our conversation had turned. I tried to move us back to safer ground. "To tell you the truth, at times I've wondered why I'm running. I'm glad the election's only a couple of weeks away."

"Thirteen days, seventeen hours, and seven minutes until I'm free," Arnold told me, smiling. Then he turned serious again. "Listen, Ralph, I know I'm dumping a lot on you at once but I am worried. As I see it, you have a ninety percent chance of winning, but this is politics. It can go in any direction. Right now Gus is spreading lies about you. Even worse, he's aiming at your family."

"I have lived through that before," I reminded him. "When I showed up my first year with Angie, the country was being torn apart over civil rights. Then I show up here with an African-American wife. It got pretty vicious."

"This is a little different," Arnold told me. "Gus says you all are secret Mormons, you and your two wives."

"That's just plain silly," I said. "I have no desire to become a Mormon. Mother Allison is a house guest until she finds a place she likes better. She's a big help to Rose with Rick when she's there, which is not all the time."

"She's been a big help with my wife, too," Arnold said. "This has all been pretty rough on her."

I was so lost in thought I almost missed the next thing Arnold said. "I'm sorry, my mind took off like a scared rabbit. I didn't catch what you said."

"I was saying that most people I know are aware of the large gifts you've given to the town over the years."

"Those were supposed to be anonymous!"

Arnold grinned. "They were, for a while. But this is a small town. Things kind of leak out a little at a time and after a while most folk get the picture. The point is, you are well thought of around here, Ralph, and I have some surprises for little boy Gus, myself."

"Like what?" I asked, immediately concerned and not knowing why.

"That's for me to know and for you to find out," he said with a cryptic grin. "Don't worry about it."

"Come on, Arnold. I need to know. I insist."

Arnold glared at me, then gave me another evil grin. "Like how he plays his horn," he said, still quite cryptic. "Bottom line, it's none of your damn business. It's between me and God and my confessor. What you don't know won't hurt you."

It was clear there was no way I was going to move him, so we talked a while about other things. When I left, Arnold told me not to be a stranger and asked if I would stop by again. I promised him I would the very next week, and I promised to bring him one of Cody's books, inscribed by the author. That tickled him.

Ali was home that evening and I told her about my visit with Arnold. When I told her what he said about his confessor, she smiled in an odd way and nodded. It was then I understood that she was the confessor Arnold had been talking about.

Seeing this dawn on me, Ali smiled again and said nothing. When I said, "I hope he doesn't do anything too outrageous," she simply shrugged.

"Arnold was right, you know," she told me gently. "It really is none of your business. It's between him and his confessor and God."

It was four days later that Ali got a call in the wee hours of the morning. "That was about Arnold Sahlberg," she told us with tears in her eyes. "His wife just found him. He died peacefully in his sleep."

When I heard this I was sad I was not able to keep my promise to Arnold. Then, almost three weeks later, the significance of when Arnold died finally struck me. For he was still the County Tax Collector when he had passed on before the end of his term. His death made four tax collectors who died in office. The odd thing was that I was in the middle of being sworn in when I realized this. I wondered if I would be the fifth.

9

Public Service

Winning the election turned our lives upside down at first. My time was no longer my own and I had made some promises I intended to keep. I told myself this would not be for long. The regular election was in a year and a half and I intended to spend my time getting the office turned around and running smoothly. This would mean we could not pick up and go as we had been doing.

To make a smooth transition I intended to promote the senior office assistant to office manager right away. Yet Ali warned me against moving too fast. It was my first day as Tax Collector and the three of us were having breakfast.

"There's a reason Arnold didn't do this already," Ali pointed out. "You might want to talk with his widow first. Or, better yet, ask Rose to drop by and find out."

I thought about that a moment. "Why not you?" I asked. "She knows you." Rose nodded.

"Yes, but I'm her pastor," Ali reminded me. "She may go to the Lutheran church but she and I really connected when I reached out to Arnold. So she goes there to worship but she comes to me for counsel. So there would be confidentiality issues. Not to mention a conflict of interest. Rose is your wife. So people will respond to her that way. They will probably tell her things they want you to know but aren't willing to tell you themselves."

"Plausible deniability," Rose said with a grimace.

I reached out and took Ali's hand. "That all makes sense but I want something to be quite clear in your mind, woman.

You are my wife, too."

"Little pitchers," Ali reminded me gently. Rick was lying in Rose's arms watching us intently. "We need to come up with something else. W-i-f-e or s-p-o-u-s-e needs to be limited to Rose."

"I don't know what to suggest," I said. "All the synonyms I know tend to be pejorative. We need to keep it something respectable."

"I always liked odalisque," Ali said smiling. "As long as the seraglio is limited to two."

"My, aren't we getting literary," Rose replied. "But I agree. More than two would be a crowd. What's wrong with Aunt Ali? Or would you prefer Ali?"

"Now that would get them talking, wouldn't it?" Ali said, her arms raised like Rocky. Rick liked this and raised his arms like she did. "You're the real champ around here, aren't you, stinkpot?" She buzzed her lips at him. He gurgled and raised his arms again and broke wind.

"He's certainly his father's child, isn't he?" Rose said, pinching her nose and Ali laughed.

"One of the privileges of ancient age," I assured them. "I hate to break this up but I need to be on time my first day."

It felt odd driving to work at an office again after so many years being semi-retired. I stopped at the bakery and picked up a dozen different pastries. All the staff were already there when I walked in a minute past eight, with one obvious exception. They seemed a bit nervous, like a flock of chickens when they spot a hawk soaring over their pen. I understood why. County jobs are hard to get in rural areas. They tend to have tenure, as well.

"Where's Gus?" I asked and they all looked down. I let the silence grow heavy until the youngest clerk finally spoke up. "He called in sick today, sir."

"Did you take the call, Gwen?" I asked. She had been one of my students several years before but she looked much different than I remembered.

"No, Doctor Williams," she said, glancing at the senior clerk before lapsing into silence.

I turned to the senior clerk, a stocky woman named Wanda Dreck. "How about you, Wanda?" She nodded but said nothing. "What did he tell you?"

Wanda studied an invisible spot on the floor. "Just that he was feeling sick," she told me, still not looking at me.

"I know this must be tough for you," I told them. "I wish Arnold Sahlberg was here instead of me. I didn't get a chance to know him as well as I would have liked, but he was good people. The attendance at his funeral is a good indication of that."

I don't like cliches. So I paused trying to think of a better way to say what I needed to get across. Yet I could not and I plunged ahead, flank speed and damn the bromides.

"Even so, life has to go on. I learned that when Angie died. So what I would like to see us do is pull together. We're here to serve the pubic and I want you to keep that in mind in every thing you do. We need to be fair and we need to be courteous, even when the people we serve are not."

I paused, gathering my thoughts. "This means there will be some very simple rules. Gwen can write these down and keep the master list. I'd like for you all to read it first thing at work every morning. That's rule number one." I smiled and Gwen smiled back. Wanda didn't and our third clerk, Lucille looked very uncertain.

"These are off the top of my head and we may need to revise them as we go," I continued. "The second rule is that I do not want you to ever argue with anyone, even if they are dead wrong. That goes double for any disagreements among staff members. We do not air our dirty laundry in public. If there is a disagreement, call me or the office manager right away. Let one of us handle it. That's a big part of our job, being the flak catchers."

"Third, you all know your jobs better than I do. I trust you to do them as best you can and I will do all I can not to micro-manage. I will be hiring an office manager within the next few weeks. His or her job will be to help you do your job as effectively as you can but without joggling your elbow. Do you have all this, Gwen?"

"Yes, sir," she answered, holding up a steno book.

"Good. I think that will help us get started. Does anyone have any questions?" No one responded. "All, right, if you think of one later, I will be in the office all day, all week. When my door is open, you are welcome to come in and talk."

Then I had another thought. "How about burning issues? Does anyone have one to burn?" I made a point of smiling. Once again, no one spoke up and I continued. "All right, then. Who is in charge of job descriptions?"

The clerks looked at each other. It was Gwen who finally said, "That would be Gus, sir."

"All right, does anyone know where he keeps these? I need to start going through them." Everyone looked at Wanda and I asked if she would bring them to me.

"He keeps them locked up," Wanda told me. Her tone was just short of being surly.

"Does anyone else have a key?" I asked, looking around the group. Everyone shook their heads. I got the impression that Wanda was not telling the truth but there was little I could do about it at the moment.

"All right. Who handles incoming calls?" Gwen raised her hand. "Call the locksmith and ask him to come in. Tell him it's for the whole office and needs to be done today, if possible."

Wanda looked shocked. "That will need approval from the County Commissioners. They'll want bids."

"I'll pay for it out of my discretionary fund," I told her. Looking at Gwen, I said, "Make the call. Tell them we're paying cash and it's high priority." Turning to Wanda, I said, "Let's talk."

My first conversation with Wanda was very difficult. She seemed determined to thwart me any way she could. She was smart enough to never challenge me directly or give me cause for summary dismissal, but she was an avatar of passive aggression.

Even so, I didn't challenge her on this which I think surprised her. I think she took it as a sign of weakness, which was a mistake. Once it was clear to me that she was determined to be obstructive I decided that our meeting was a waste of time. What I needed was evidence that would hold up in court if Wanda chose to sue, and it would take a while to gather and organize this. So I told her we would talk later.

I made a point of going by the other offices in the courthouse to introduce myself the second afternoon I was in office. However, the sheriff was gone and I dropped by his office the next morning to pay my respects. The first thing he asked me was how Gus was working out.

"I don't know," I told him. "He's been out all week with post-election flu."

The sheriff nodded. "I'm not surprised. How about Wanda?"

"Aside from trying to sabotage everything I want to accomplish and trying to intimidate the rest of the staff?" I asked. "She's the soul of sweetness and light."

The sheriff shrugged and nodded his sympathy. "One thing you need to know is that she and Gus are in cahoots."

"I figured as much," I told him. "I think she must have a crush on him."

"Oh, it's far more than that," the sheriff said. "It has been for a long time now. They have been seen getting it on here and there around the county." He handed me a file. "That's what I have, chapter and verse. You're welcome to look at it or copy it but I need to hang onto the original."

I took the file without opening it. "Are they aware you have this?" I asked.

The sheriff shook his head. "They seem to think no one knows. To tell you the truth, what you have there would not stand up in court. At least, not without a smoking gun or at least supporting evidence."

"Was Arnold Sahlberg aware of this?" I asked.

"I think he may have been but Wanda is one of his wife's cousins. Not by blood but by marriage. I think he decided not to know too much until he had to do something. He's a pretty smart man - I mean he was - and I'm sure he was aware that most flings don't last more than a couple of years. I think he was hoping that Gus and Wanda would bust up, at least at first. To tell you the truth, I'm surprised it's lasted at least five years and still seems to be going strong."

"I know Gus is married. How about Wanda?"

The sheriff looked embarrassed. "She is and adultery is a gross misdemeanor. I know because I looked it up when Arnold asked me about it. The statute is still on the books, number 609.36 if you need to know. It isn't enforced much these days, thank God, or I'd be snowed under. So I knew Arnold was aware of it. I kept expecting him to do something but he never did. I decided if he wasn't going to push it, I wouldn't, either. That may be wrong but that's how I saw it."

The sheriff glanced down and studied the floor. "The thing is, Wanda is my wife's first cousin, too, and she comes from a big clan. I wouldn't have won the election without their support. I'm not proud of it but there it is. She's kinfolks."

"So I'm on my own?"

"Oh, no," the sheriff told me and there was resolve in his voice. "You won't be the only one running in the general election in eighteen months, but I'll do the right thing. You have my word on that. However, you are the one who has to take point. I won't make a move until you do."

"Fair enough," I told him. "She is my problem, after all. I need to get her out of the office until the auditor is done but I'm not sure how to approach it. I think I'll put her on paid administrative leave for a while but I think everyone might be better off if she was gone for good. Wanda included."

"Looking at the way you handled your campaign, I'd be surprised if you don't figure it out pretty quick."

I nodded. "I think I need to start with paid leave to get her out of the office. Gus, I think, I will just fire."

"That may be easier said than done," the sheriff told me. "He's been here a long time and the County Commissioners will almost certainly be involved. Your case better be airtight."

"Maybe the auditor will turn up something," I said. "I would hate to fire him on moral grounds. I don't want to ruin his life. I just want him to go away. There's Wanda to consider, too."

The sheriff nodded. "I think the auditor would be your best chance. I expect Gus has been as sloppy with public funds as he has with the election and his love life. So your ammunition is most likely out there. You just need to find it."

"I don't suppose there are federal funds involved, are there?"

The sheriff was startled but then he grinned. "You don't

mess around, do you? I'll look around and keep my ears open. It would be handy to let the feds take the heat. Save us both some trouble."

"Don't get your hopes too high, Sheriff. That would be too easy."

On my way back to the office I thought about what the sheriff said. This had jogged something loose in the gray cells and gave me an idea. I'd asked all the clerks to write up a detailed list of their actual duties and to meet with me to discuss these. Since Gus was not at work, I'd also asked each of them to write up her understanding of how Gus actually spent his time.

So far I had talked with Wanda only once and quite briefly. To date she had not finished the assignment I'd given on the first day. Nor had she been able to produce a job description for Gus. She claimed that other duties had prevented her doing so and mentioned several reports still on her desk.

I had also talked with Lucille Mueller. She was a tall, pleasant lady in her late forties who seemed very timid. Even so, she had been quite candid with me about Gus when no one else was present. I took careful notes of what she said but all she had were allegations, not evidence of wrong doing. "Ask Gwen," Lucille told me. "If anyone has the cold facts it would be her."

That morning it was time to talk to Gwen. I asked her if she had finished her assignment and she told me she had. Nor was she working on anything that could not wait. So I asked her to bring her work description to my office along with the assignment.

Once Gwen was seated I asked how long she had worked in the tax office. She told me it had been almost seven years by then. "Surely not," I said, smiling to reassure her. "It seems only like yesterday we were discussing Hamlet. As I recall, yours was the best essay in the class. As a matter of fact, it was one of the best I have ever read."

"I don't know about that, Doctor Williams, but you did give me an A+." I could see she was pleased that I had remembered. I noticed there was no ring on her finger and I wondered why she didn't do more to make herself look attractive. I also wondered why she was blushing.

"Maybe we better keep it Mister Williams here at the office," I told her and she nodded. "Am I wrong in thinking you and Lucille look out for each other?"

"Yes, sir, we're friends. We do a lot of stuff together." Her eyes were lowered when she said this and once again I wondered what was going on. I remembered her as a far more assertive student.

"Well, it's good to have a friend at the office. Just to put your mind at rest, I am aware of the situation with Gus and Wanda. I've been told by a reliable source that they are an item, so to speak, and have been for years. I'm not going to put you on the spot asking about that. What I need for you to do for me right now is to talk about his absences from the office. Is there any way of documenting these?"

"Yes, sir, I keep a work log for everybody who works here. Mister Sahlberg told me to do that not long before he got sick."

This put a whole new face on the situation. It looked like Arnold was more aware of what was going on than I had thought. "What about when you're gone? Who keeps tabs on things then?"

"That's me and I'm never gone, Doctor - I'm sorry - Mister Williams."

"You're never sick or on vacation?"

"Not since I started keeping the work record."

"So does Gus tell you where he's going?"

"Yes, sir, he always tells me. At least he did up until Arnie - Mister Sahlberg got really sick six months ago. After that he just came and went without saying a word." She shrugged.

"Did you make a note of this?" I asked.

Gwen nodded. "Yes, sir. I logged the time he left and how long he was gone. I always put down a couple of question marks when he didn't tell me where he was going. I logged his returns, too."

"Did you ever ask him to fill in the blank periods?"

"Only once, Mister Williams. He got pretty mad and yelled at me when I did. So I didn't do it again."

"But you still kept track, anyway, didn't you?" She smiled and nodded and I thought about this. "Did Arnold ask you to keep track of anyone else?"

"Yes, sir, all of us, but Lucille and I didn't go out any except to run office errands. I did log these."

"Excellent!" I told her. "You did a good job. Keep it up, including my time. I need you to make a copy of your log and give it to me. I also need you to keep the log under lock and key. Do you have a secure area in your desk?"

"I do now," she told me. "I hope I wasn't wrong but I asked the locksmith to only make two keys for the top drawer of my desk. I also asked him to do the same thing for your desk. I hope that was all right."

"Excellent! I'll need one set of the keys. The new office manager will have to have copies but you keep them for now."

Gwen started to say something else but stopped. "Yes, Gwen?" I asked. "Go ahead."

Gwen looked down again. "I don't know if it's all right or not, sir. I don't want to give offense but would you consider promoting someone from in the office?"

"Look at me, Gwen," I said. "Are you asking to be the new office manager or are you suggesting Lucille? Wanda is definitely not in the running."

Gwen snorted and covered her mouth, blushing bright red when she did. "Sorry, sir."

"Two things, Gwen. I remember you from class as being a lot more assertive. You strike me now as a little too meek. This job is going to need someone who can be hard nosed and courteous at the same time. Can you do that?"

Gwen sat up in her chair and looked me in the eye. The change was startling. "Of course, I can!" she declared. "Why do you think Arnie gave the log to me rather than to Lucille?"

I nodded my approval. This was the Gwen I knew as a student. "I'm surprised that Gus didn't take them away from you."

"He tried to but I insisted he put it in writing and to get Mr. Sahlberg to sign off on it. He backed off but a couple of weeks later the log disappeared from my desk one night. It was in a locked drawer but it didn't look like anyone pried it open. It's a steel desk just like yours, so whoever took it had to have a key."

"You mean it's gone?"

"No, sir. I thought that might happen so I kept a copy of everything. The original is locked in my desk right now and I have an electronic backup. What was taken was some duplicate records we were about to shred."

"All right, Gwen. That's very good work. You have six weeks to make it or break it as our interim office manager. In the meantime I will be interviewing other applicants for the job. Understand, I have to do this under the law. If you qualify and are promoted, whoever I hire will be your assistant. That is only with your approval. I don't think Lucille has what it takes."

"You're absolutely correct, sir. She's very good doing her current job but she needs clear direction. When she needs help she comes to me. I don't think she'll apply."

"It sounds like you're the one who's been keeping the office running."

"As best as I could, sir. There were some things I couldn't do without getting fired and I need the job."

"Would I be off base asking why? It's none of my business but I'd like to know."

"It's all right, sir. I have a daughter. I've been raising her on my own. I don't get child support."

I thought about this for a moment. "None of this is my business, Gwen. I hope you understand this. I do hope that if you ever get in a jam you'll come to me. I mean that. Not as your boss but as your friend."

"Yes, sir," she said, fighting back the tears that came out of nowhere.

"All right, then. Let's go over your work summary but call a staff meeting for one o'clock when we're done. I will let everyone know you're the interim office manager. If anyone gives you any guff about it, refer them directly to me."

Gwen smiled. "Thank you, sir but I won't have to. I'll get you the keys. And an application and resume, too." She smiled sweetly.

The office meeting went about as well as I expected. For privacy we moved into the small conference room used for extra space. I put a note on the entry door that said the office would open again at one-thirty.

"We don't have a lot to cover so I'll get right down to the nitty gritty," I told them. "I understand that it's customary to use first names among the staff. When it's just us chickens, we will continue that practice. So I'll be Ralph. Yet, when we are talking to members of the public, however, we will use the person's title and last name, and our own. This is much more courteous and it reinforces the attitude that we are professionals here to serve them. If you don't know who the person is, use 'sir' or 'miz' regardless of the age of the women. Any questions?"

There was no response. "Second, we will be hiring an office manager and at least one other clerk in the next few weeks. Gwen will be the interim office manager. She will also be considered for that job permanently. Her first task will be to meet with each of you and talk about your duties. She will also be your supervisor. Are there any questions about that?"

"She doesn't have seniority!" Wanda protested. "She isn't old enough."

I was expecting this, of course, and I met the issue head on. "First of all, any promotions during my term in office will be on merit, not longevity or age. Second, the position requires loyalty. I have known Gwen for several years and I need someone I can trust."

"That's not fair!" Wanda protested. "I've worked here more than twenty-five years."

"Yes, and that's why you still have a job, Wanda. I asked my attorney to research the statutes. As long as you perform your job reasonably well in a professional manner and do not break the law, you will remain part of our staff. You may or may not be doing the same tasks you are doing now but you will have a job at the same pay grade."

I paused to see if Wanda had anything else to say but she only glared at me. I looked at Gwen and she shrugged. Then I looked at Lucille who seemed to be quite frightened. I smiled to reassure her.

I told Wanda that she and I and Gwen needed to talk. I asked Lucille if she would tend the phone and front desk until we were done. She nodded gratefully and rushed out of the room.

"All right, Wanda, we need to get down to brass tacks. Do you want to keep working here?" I asked. Wanda glared at me but gave me a curt nod.

"All right, then, would you like to wait and talk about this until you feel more calm?" Again, she gave me a curt nod.

"Very well. I am going to put you on paid leave for the next few days. What I want you to do is to figure out if there's any way we can work together. You have until a week from Friday to call us back and let me or Gwen know. Just remember that if you do not call I will assume you're telling us the answer is 'no' and that you are resigning. So the ball is in your court. Is that clear?" Wanda nodded.

I looked at our new office manager. "Do you have anything to add, Gwen?" She shook her head.

When Wanda had left the office I asked Gwen to stay behind and closed the door. "Any conversations with Wanda been to be held when you and I are both present or on the line, Either that or they need to be recorded. Do you know how to do that on our phone here?"

"Yes," she told me. "I have an archive of phone calls with her or Gus which I recorded to protect myself. Do you want them?"

"Only if there are any you think I need to hear. I really don't like having to do this, Gwen. Is there any other issue we need to discuss?" She shook her head and I added, "Good. I'm going to step across the street and drown my sorrows in a bowl of ice cream."

Gwen laughed and was still smiling when I got back a half hour later. Then it was time to get down to basics of how our office was supposed to work.

My ladies gave me the third degree, of course, when I got home that evening. The details of our meeting with Wanda hit the gossip chain with minimal distortion and made it around the county at lightning speed. By the time I got home the phone was ringing. "Its one of the county commissioners," Rose told me. "He sounds very unhappy." She looked worried.

I took the phone and pushed the record button. When I identified myself the person on the other end launched into a tirade about how I was running my office. "Who am I talking to?" I asked and this precipitated another tirade. I recognized the voice but I repeated the question.

"This is Bud Hicks!" the voice finally snarled.

"Well, Mister Hicks, you're welcome to come by the office and discuss this tomorrow," I told him. "None of it sounds much like an emergency and dinner is family time for us."

This precipitated a torrent of profanity and I waited until it was done. "You do realize, of course, that this is a one party consent state," I informed him.

"What in the hell does that mean?"

"It means I am legally recording this conversation. I hope you don't talk that way in front of your grandkids." There was dead silence on the other end of the line followed by a sudden click.

I hung up and gave my family a hug. "I think we need a second line," I told my ladies. "One that's not listed." They both nodded.

"Let's talk about it after supper," Rose suggested.

"Of course," I answered. "First things first. I want to know about your days, too."

This became our pattern during my years as county tax collector. It became a ritual of homecoming and a way of staying in touch that we observed rigorously. It was our way of getting rid of the garbage *du jour* and keeping it away from our family table.

That third evening on the job as the four of us sat in front of the fire Ali told me she knew of two very good book keepers from the reservation. "They refer to each other as sisters," she told us. "Translated to the English way of looking at things, that means cousins. Both of them are as sharp as tack and one of them is studying for her CPA."

"Sounds good to me," I replied. "A little affirmative action would be good. I don't suppose they would consider working as temps first, would they? What are their names?"

When Ali told me, I laughed. "I apparently have a very efficient office manager. Just before I left she told me she had called them in for an interim interview. That's tomorrow afternoon."

"What about Gus?" Rose asked. "What are you going to do about him?"

"I'm going to fire him if I can. I was looking at his absentee record this afternoon and he has been absent from the office without accounting for it ever since Arnie had to quit coming in. I think his work record alone is probably enough to carry most of the county commissioners. I'm sure Bud Hicks will be a problem."

"Sounds like you need to do some schmoozing with your board members," Rose said.

"For sure," Ali agreed. "You need to be proactive, too. You need to tackle them one at a time and make them your friends. Then you need to stay tight with them. They're already on your side."

"What do you mean? They don't know me from Adam, Ali."

"Sure they do," she asserted. "You've been here over thirty years and you've been very generous. They all know this, even Bud."

All of sudden I remembered my conversation with Arnold. He had told me my anonymous gifts here and there had gradually leaked and were public knowledge. I was so caught up in the thought that I missed the next thing Ali said. "Sorry," I told her. "I missed that."

"I said they were impressed by the letters."

"What letters?" I asked.

"You didn't see them?" Ali asked, dumbfounded.

"I didn't see what?"

Ali and Rose both broke up laughing. It was Rose who answered my question.

"Arnold's letters of endorsement, sweetie. He sent them out just before he died. He spelled it out, chapter and verse. He told them about Gus' dishonesty and his abuse of his position."

"Mostly he told them about your generous gifts and how you insisted that they be kept anonymous," Ali added. "The board is on your side, dear man."

"Arnie told me he was going to do something but he wouldn't tell me what," I said. "I kept worrying about dirty tricks that never happened."

"So seek them out, one by one," Ali said. "Ask them what they think you should do about Gus. About Wanda, too."

Rose nodded. "You'll win their respect," she said. "Even Bud Hicks. So don't forget him."

So I followed the wisdom of my women and they were absolutely right. I sought out each of the board members and showed them Gus' work record over the last six months. I told them about the file of letters of complaint Gwen had put together from Arnold's filing cabinet at home. Then I asked each of them what they thought needed to be done. Seven out of our eight commissioners, responded pretty much the same. Bud Hicks was the only exception.

"I'd fire his ass if he worked for me," one of them, a general contractor, put it bluntly.

"You can't afford someone like that on the team," one of the local grocers told me. "People like that are bad for morale. We don't pay that much, as it is, but one thing we can offer is a good work environment."

"I don't know," the lone dissenter said. "He's been there a long time. You think he really deserves it? You know what people will say, that it's purely political."

"Are you kidding, Bud?" the contractor growled when this came up at the board meeting. "If he doesn't deserve it, then nobody does."

"What about Wanda?" the dissenter asked. "You going to fire her, too?"

"I wouldn't recommend that," I jumped in. "I am hoping we can get Wanda turned around. That is, unless the auditor turns up something way off base. She's not that far from retirement and if we can't work with her, I would rather see us offer her an early out incentive she can't afford to refuse."

"Couldn't she work in some other department?" the road supervisor asked. "I know she can run a grader."

"You really want to put her at the wheel of twenty tons of steel and gravel?" the contractor asked and all the others laughed.

"Not as sore as she is right now," one of the others said, speaking up for the first time and the rest sobered up right away. The speaker was the funeral director.

"She's on extended leave right now," I said. "Gwen found a couple of temps to cover the office until things settle down. So give it some thought, if you would."

"It sounds like most of us think we need to fire Gus," the owner of the laundry and cry cleaner said. "I need to get home so could we take a vote?" No one else said anything for a moment. Wilbur rarely spoke at County Commission meetings and the others were surprised.

"I do, too, Wilbur," the contractor agreed. "I move we fire Gus immediately with no benefits. We've already paid him six months to loaf."

The chair put it to an immediate vote and I was very surprised to see the lone dissenter make it unanimous. He told me later that the reason he did was what I said about trying to rehabilitate Wanda.

I had cause to be glad, but that night I drove home with a heavy heart. There was no question in my mind that Gus was a brass plated asshole who deserved exactly what had happened to him. Even so, the words of John Donne haunted me, as they always have. They reminded me that none of us is an island. There are reasons we are the way we are, for good or for ill. Nor is there any question in my mind that the One who rules the whole Universe loves his child, Gus, every step of the way, as he does with any other among us. Ali assured me I was right.

While a child of God he might be, getting fired did not sit well with Gus. I don't think it does with most people but Gus raised a ruckus. He threatened to sue me, the county commissioners, and anyone even remotely connected to the tax office.

The problem was that he could not find anyone local who was willing to represent him. Not even the bottom feeder from the Cities he talked into looking at the case wanted anything to do with it. One of our local attorneys told Gus flat out that he would be lucky to get off lightly, if at all. The outside auditor had come up with any number of irregularities in his travel expense claims, and there were forty-seven hundred dollars of public funds he had access to which were apparently missing.

The board of commissioners held a special meeting to

decide what to do about this. The commissioners were very angry about the situation and the initial consensus was to prosecute Gus to the full extent of the law. Yet the district attorney advised against it. He pointed out that it was very unlikely that any of the missing funds would ever be recovered. Even if they were, the cost of a public trial would be far greater than anything they could recover.

What the district attorney suggested was a plea bargain in which Gus agreed to first of all pay back the missing funds plus interest over a two year period and, second, to remove himself from the county and to reside not less than a hundred miles from the county courthouse. He was further forbidden from traveling to or through the county except by written permission of the court. Failure to meet these conditions would result in his being imprisoned for a minimum of five years.

When Gus tried to argue about these terms, the district attorney pointed out that he had no fewer that twenty counts of malfeasance to pursue if Gus refused the plea bargain. He also pointed out that the judge could sentence Gus to serve each count consecutively. On advice of his legal counsel, Gus finally agreed and was given ten days to get out of town.

One upshot Gus had not considered, however, was how his wife, Irma, might respond to all this. Nor was she at all reluctant to launder his dirty laundry in public and the story was all over town like a flash. Irma had told her husband that the plea bargain did not apply to her, and she could see no reason to leave town. She was well thought of in the community and the house they inhabited had been left to her by her parents. She intended to keep living there.

Irma also informed Gus that she would be seeking a divorce. Even though Minnesota was a no-fault state when it came to divorce, adultery was still on the books as a statute.

Irma said she would bring charges for every instance of his infidelities if he balked or even challenged her.

That was Gus. Wanda was a different matter. She called me back the day before the deadline and told me she would be back at the office the following Monday. She was there on time, well dressed, but it was quite apparent her attitude toward me had not changed. So I asked her into my office and asked Gwen to sit in and take notes on our meeting. I also recorded the whole conversation.

"What would you like to do, Wanda? I see three options at this point. One is for you to work here and for us to work out our differences. Another is for you to work at another county office. The third is to work out an early retirement settlement. I am also open to other choices."

"I got a lot of time with the county," she told us. "I worked for the extension office for a while and for the sheriff's office as a dispatcher. I had to work nights there so I come here as soon as I could. I figure I got twenty-seven years retirement coming." Her voice was neutral when she said this but there was a lot of suspicion and anger in her eyes.

I nodded. "That's correct. The problem is going to be finding you a spot at the same pay grade. Are you willing to consider retirement?"

"What are you offering?" she asked. It was not quite a snarl, but her answer bordered on contempt.

"We could pay you for your vacation time and give you a full retirement."

"That ain't nothing," Wanda said. "I got that coming already."

"No, according to our records you're a little over three years short. Your sick time and vacation would not quite make it thirty years. So what we are offering is three years' salary plus vacation and sick leave as severance."

Wanda glowered at me but said nothing. "I also asked around to see where else you could go with the county. The only place that has an opening close to your current pay grade is Zoning and Agriculture. That would involve some local travel, too, at state rates. The only other thing open right now is a lower pay grade job with Water Resources."

"Why can't I stay here?"

"In a word, attitude. We're trying to make this a positive place to work and we can't afford someone who is full of resentment. That's how I see you. Am I wrong?" Wanda looked down and said nothing. "Let me ask it another way. Are you willing to accept Gwen as your supervisor?"

Wanda snorted. Gwen and I looked at one another and I could see we had come to the same assessment. "Do you see any other alternatives, Gwen?"

"What about giving her another week on leave?" she asked me. "It's a big decision."

"Does that sound reasonable, Wanda?" I asked. She nodded and I said, "I need to hear you say 'yes' or 'no'."

"I'll take it!" Wanda snapped and stomped out of the office.

I am not sure what was in Wanda's mind when she left the office that Monday. I think she was hoping to work something out with Gus. News of his pending divorce was making the rounds and the word was that he was moving up to the Thief River Falls area. When Ali told us this, we had a laugh about how appropriate that was for him.

Even so, Wanda did not leave town. Her husband was a long distance trucker and we heard that when he was in town the next time, she had him served with divorce papers. He was heard at a local watering hole to say that wouldn't make much difference. "Hell," he added, "she's been sleeping around since we were married. What difference is that going to make? I sleep in the rig most nights, anyway."

It wasn't too long after that the rumor mill had it that John Dreck, Wanda's husband, had hit the road again, this time with a part time waitress at the truck stop. Word had it that she was twenty years younger than John and needed to get out of Dodge. It had something to do with her abusive boyfriend.

Two weeks after we talked, Wanda Dreck showed up at the office and took the commissioners' retirement offer. The next thing we heard was that she was living with some man in Grand Forks, about fifty miles west of Thief River Falls. There was no news about Gus.

10

Ralph's Epilogue

Well, that's the story of how I met the woman of my dreams, discovered a whole new side of me I never suspected was there, and became a public servant. On the way, I also found myself blessed with a gorgeous odalisque, sired a wonderful daughter with her, and found peace within my troubled self in an even more troubled world. Rose and I never did a lot of casual traveling after that first trip home from Texas and I gave up book conferences for a well extended Lent. After a while word got out that Cody Grey Adams had hung up his quill for good and all the uninvited invitations stopped. Yet it was six months before I noticed it and if my agent had not called I might never have become aware of it.

Even so, the four of us did make short expeditions here and there and we made an extended trip to Italy one fierce winter. Ali had a lot of sabbatical leave coming and the timing was perfect. Somehow the three of us had managed to knock her up, too, as she liked to say. So she and Rose flew out with Rick before she was too far along, and I joined them there a couple of months later. By then Gwen was running the office pretty much on her own but I checked in a couple of times every week. When I did it was mostly to pass along the adventures of the Williams family.

One thing I didn't pass along was that our lovely daughter decided it was time to be born on one fine spring day. So we all went to the American Consulate to register June Ellen as an American citizen. She was three years younger than her brother, Rick, but it took June-bug no time to win him over completely. He even let her boss him around.

Even so seeing June the first time almost broke my heart. There was no question she had the same tall frame and good looks as Ali, her birth mother. Yet June was the spitting image of my daughter, Carol, killed in that awful train collision so many years before.

One of the things we talked about from time to time in Italy was how we could account for showing up with a brand new baby. "Why don't we be outrageous?" Ali asked one day after a lazy lunch. "People will believe the damnedest things, so the more so, the better."

Rose and I looked at each other, not knowing what to expect. One of the things we soon learned about our beloved spouse was that she had an unpredictable wild streak that burst out of confinement every once in a while. It was a wonderful gift that kept all of us a little off balance, out of a rut. This sounded like one of those episodes of divine madness about to break forth and neither Rose nor I had any idea what Ali was about to suggest.

"What did you have in mind, love?" Rose asked.

"Oh, I don't know. I was thinking about me having a brief, passionate fling with an unidentified drummer from an equally unidentified jazz band." Ali grinned. "I think that would sell like hotcakes in Mayberry."

Mayberry was how Ali referred to our small city in northwestern Minnesota in private conversations. Lake Wobegon was another of her favorites, too. "What do you think?" Ali asked. "Is that too far over the top?"

"I think most of our friends would know you're putting them on."

Ali nodded and frowned. "Lies are most believable close to the truth," I suggested. "The strongest ones are when the truth is told in a way it won't be believed."

"Yeah," Ali said. "So what's the balls-to-the-wall truth here? That Ralph knocked Ali up higher than Ben Franklin's kite? Totally BO-ring unless you were reclined at ground zero!" She smiled at us when she said this. "At least, it would be after a couple of months."

"Boring isn't necessarily bad," I offered. "You could also be paradoxical. Say nothing until someone asks and say something like, 'I found her under a cabbage leaf.' Then wink and grin."

"You're wicked, Cody Grey Adams." Ali often called me that when I let the outrageous side of myself out to run with hers. "What if they persist?"

"Then look them in the eye and ask them what the bloody, blue BLEEP makes it any of their business."

"What about telling the simple truth?" Rose asked. "There doesn't seem much risk there. Ralph ran unopposed last year and was reelected, so he still has what, three years left in his term? He's also talking about hanging it up when it expires. You're talking about stepping down from parish work and being a full time volunteer on the reservation. People up there are a lot more accepting of babies out of wedlock. And if you're a useful volunteer, who can fire you? Who on the tribal council would want to? Or dare? The women up there are on your side."

Ali nodded and looked at me. "I think I like the cabbage leaf scenario better. It keeps them guessing and I think they might like that better." Then she looked at Rose. "Besides, people on the rez would get a good laugh out of it."

As I said, that's the story of how I met the woman of my dreams, discovered a whole new side of myself I never suspected was there, and became a public servant. This was not the life I had in mind when I met Rose. I had every reason to assume we would live a life of leisure summering on our lake in Minnesota and wintering in some warmer clime. Our time would be our own and we could play tag-team being parents to our children.

When I mentioned this to Ali one beautiful Indian summer morning in September, she chuckled. "They say that if you want to make God laugh, then tell Her your plans."

"So who is 'they' who say this?" I asked.

"Who dat who say 'who do dat?'" she replied with a grin. "What's it worth to you, big fella?"

"A kiss but I'll pay up front," I replied, giving her the same grin back and moving close.

"Mmm," she purred when we were done. "Someone is telling me you want more than that."

"That's only a faint flicker," I chuckled. "The spirit is willing but the flesh? The old fart is sound asleep."

"I bet I can wake him up," she replied, fumbling with my belt. "But to answer your question, I hear a lot of AA folk say the thing about making God laugh." She tugged at my jeans and they slipped down over my bare butt. Then she opened her eyes in mock surprise. "Well, goodness, gracious. Looky there what I found."

Later we all had a good laugh at the irony of what Ali and I had been talking about, telling God our plans. For we just happened to be alone in the house that fine September morning. Like other parents of small children, we took advantage of it. Repeatedly. That was the fall before we wintered in Italy.

11

Postscript by Rose Williams

Ralph and I had fourteen wonderful years together. He lost a lot of extra weight and we did a lot of healthy things. We exercised together, ate healthy food, and took care of ourselves. We also laughed a lot and made love every day, one way or another. Sometimes it was simply holding one another close and at other times it was watching the changes of the seasons through our picture window overlooking the lake. At other times it was when our eyes met across the room at a party or a dinner or taking a long walk down the beach those years when we wintered in warmer places.

Nor did any of this replace the physical union that has bound women and men together from the beginning. I think the way the three of us were as a partnership was what made such a union possible between us even to the week Ralph died, and it is this casual intimacy that I miss most.

I also believe that serving our community as the tax collector was also part of what added years to Ralph's life. The life of a writer has its rewards but public service day after day kept Ralph focused beyond our little life as a family. Ralph never took a penny of the salary he was entitled to receive, and he used to say that is what kept him from becoming a professional politician. He could not be bought, though many tried, and he was not dependent on his position to make a living.

I know Ralph also enjoyed the work. He kept saying he intended to step down at the end of his present term. Yet he never did. Somehow he could not help filing for office before the deadline slipped by and he was elected to an unprecedented four terms. "Me and FDR," he often said, and like his hero, he died in his fourth term. He became the fifth tax collector in a row to die in office.

The doctors told us that Ralph died of an aneurysm no one suspected was there. Nor was there anything anyone could have done. The two of us were sitting cuddled together watching the fire one evening while Ali and the kids fixed dinner. Suddenly Ralph told me he had a really bad headache and asked me to bring him an aspirin. When I got back less than a minute later he was slumped on the couch right where I had left him. At first I thought he had fallen asleep. There was a very peaceful look on his face and I almost left him there to rest. Something made me touch his hand and I knew he was gone, even before I tried to find a pulse. The vessel that carried him through this world was empty and what had made him Ralph Williams, and Cody Grey Adams, as well, had moved on to a greater reality.

What came to mind as I thought about it later were the words of that gospel hymn Ralph loved so well, I'll Fly Away. Ralph once told me it was one of his father-in-law's favorite hymns, too, and even the most staid of the Norwegians among whom we lived were deeply moved when the gospel choir cut loose singing it at his memorial service. The five of us had been to the Cities as often as we could to hear the choir. We had come to know them like extended family, and I was amazed how much joy I felt despite my loss. Mixed in with all this was the gratitude I felt having met this wonderful man. The world was less without him in it.

As Ralph mentioned earlier, he and I had one child, Richard. He was born nine months to the day from when we met at the writer's conference in Austin. While this might have cramped our lifestyle, it did not. We took Rick everywhere we went together and our life revolved around family. At Ralph's urging, bordering on insistence, I finished my degree at The University of Texas in Austin. Yet I never pursued English any further, though I did pinch hit as a faculty substitute at the university where Ralph had taught. Later, I followed my passion and earned a certificate in culinary arts. I became a chef with a clientele of four plus whomever might show up for supper.

After Ralph died Ali and I finished raising our son, along with his sister June. One thing Rick and I continued was our family tradition of cooking and hosting gourmet dinners. June was always willing to help but music was her passion. The four of us were frequently asked to do food for things like weddings and other celebrations, and this eventually evolved into a catering business. So by the time he graduated from high school, Rick was well trained in culinary arts.

Unlike many of his cohorts who were anxious to attend universities all over the country, Rick elected to attend the local university where Ralph taught so many years. His goal was to learn what he needed to learn in our business school and to develop our culinary service into a full time enterprise. So by the time he had his degree Rick was well versed in down to earth business management. He was at the top of his class and it was only at my insistence that he agreed to sell this business and to enroll in the Culinary Institute of America. Having had enough of Minnesota winter, he chose to attend their San Antonio campus and was delighted when Ali and I elected to winter there the two years he was in school.

As for this manuscript, it has a story of its own. Ralph gave it to me a couple of years before he died. It is the story of our love, the three of us, and he left the decision whether or not to publish it to me and Ali. I decided the story is too wonderful to keep to ourselves and Ali agreed. We published it the year before Ralph died. As always, it was published under his pen name, Cody Grey Adams, and it was well received.

The book even won a major national award but Ralph was gone by then. So I accepted it in his name and the whole family came along for the occasion. We had a great time in New York, mostly cruising good restaurants. It was the book that paid for this, as if it was our reward for taking the time and trouble to make the trip. Yet the best reward for me was the look on Ralph's face when the first copy arrived at home. I asked him to autograph it for us. This was not long before he died and I asked him to sign it as Cody Grey Adams, AKA Bellowing Bull. Ali thought this was a hoot.

There a couple of other thing which I need to touch on before I quit and send this along to the publisher for the second addition. The canons of creative writing insist that a story must have a beginning, a middle, and an end. I am not so sure about this. I believe the story of our love will never have an end. Like the emerald rings Ali and I still wear on our fingers, every point is connected to any other an infinite number of ways. So the beginning becomes the middle becomes the end and all return to the beginning or the middle or the end, however one chooses to go.

That must be as confusing to you, the reader, as much as it is to me. Maybe I need to keep it simple and say that all things return to their beginning, including this story. It began with a simple statement: "She was the woman of my dreams." Everything else goes forth from, and returns to that beginning, which was what Cody whispered to Grace Adams so long ago in the hallway. "You are the woman of my dreams."

As softly as Cody spoke, I still heard those words. Yet I

never told Cody how they cut me to the heart. I felt so jealous hearing him say this I could hardly bear it. For I knew I could make his dreams come true in ways Grace could never imagine. Over the fourteen years we had together I never, stopped trying to do exactly that, to make our love as full as it could be. With Ralph's help, and Ali's, too, I believe I was able to do so. So did Ralph and those were his last words, "You, Rose, are the woman of my dreams."

Oddly enough, I ran into Grace Adams the second year we wintered in San Antonio. I was enjoying the River Walk one warm afternoon, minding my own business. I was sharing the moment with Ralph, as I often do. So I never saw Grace coming until it was to late to avoid her. She apparently never knew Ralph and I had married or that Cody Grey Adams was Ralph's pen name.

"Rose?" someone asked and I looked around. I saw a well dressed woman to whom the years had not been kind. Even though she was fifteen years younger than I, her countenance was drawn and pinched. It was the embodiment of the opening words of King Richard III. "Now is the winter of our discontent...," the bard wrote and this was etched all over her face, so much that I did not recognize her. It was clear her days had not been pleasant or fulfilling.

"Rose Williams?" the woman asked again, then rushed on. "I'm Grace, Grace Adams. We used to be roommates a long time ago."

I was so shocked seeing what life had done to Grace I could not respond for a moment. "I guess none of us look like we did," she continued.

I could sense the woman was very nervous and I could not see why she had spoken to me. Surely she had not forgotten the bitterness of our last encounter. "Yes," I said, not knowing what else to say. "It's been so long I didn't recognize you." I was careful to keep my tone neutral and my feelings shut deep in my heart.

Grace took my polite response as forgiveness or at least permission to inflict herself on my presence. She plopped her considerable self down on the other end of the bench where I sat. I heard bolts groan against the wooden slats when she did and I hoped they did not give way before the assault of her sizable mass. "What in the world have you been up to?" Grace asked. Then, before I could answer, she launched into what she had to say.

Among other things, Grace had a much different sense of what went down at the conference than I did. She told me Cody Grey, as she called him, had sought her out a month after the Austin writer's conference and that they had become secret lovers for years. She also claimed to be the woman of his dreams and that she was the woman called Rosemarie in the first edition. Then she began to render her account of their secret trysts in some of the better known watering holes of the international jet set.

Had it not been so pathetic I would have challenged Grace but I saw stark fear in her eyes. It was a fear that expected to be fulfilled in shame and rejection and I simply could not do it. I remembered what Ralph had to say about the couple we had lunch with in Fort Worth, how empty their lives were in the quiet desperation that filled their days. Except for the quiet part, that was Grace.

So I did not disabuse her of her fantasy or even argue the facts. Nor was I sure this was the kindest thing I could have done for her, to sustain the lie she lived. So I talked to Ralph about it that night. I have talked to him like that almost every day since he died. It's always a monologue, of course, but the day I talked to him about Grace it felt like he was sitting right there beside me.

My sense of Ralph's response was interesting. He pointed out that it was Cody who was responsible for her delusion in the first place. She was not entirely at fault. His sin was placing his needs ahead of hers.

I tried to argue but Ralph asked me to let it go. Then he played dirty pool, speaking the truth rather than sustaining the lie. He reminded me of an old love song we both knew well and reminded me of an earlier conversation about it. "You see, love," he said gently. "All she's got are her fantasies," he pointed out, "lesser things, but I've got you and you have me. And if you don't know it by now, you are the woman of my dreams, just like I talked about at the conference. You have always been so and so you will always be."

Then I could almost see Ralph grin. "As for the old bellowing bull in Austin? He just had a little of dust in his eyes at first, my love. He was blinded by lust and mistook her for you. After all, who was the one he chose to mate?"

As I close this testament, there is a significant omission I need to correct here. This is about our beloved friend and partner, Allison. As you may have noticed, neither Ralph nor I has ever set down her last name. This has been mostly to protect both her and June while Ali was in active parish ministry. Now at this season of life there is little need. Ali hung up her collar years ago and long before she did Ralph set up a trust for her and another for June so they could be independent. Even from us, should she so choose, as he put it. Yet Ali never so chose and the trust has gone to June.

When her service at our home parish was done Ali chose to become what she called a gypsy priest, serving were she was needed. Yet she was never so far away that she could not come home every week. A lot of her work was on the reservations not far from us and among the Lakota she became known as the *Winyan Wakan*, the holy woman. It was hard work, emotionally, and she often said we were the haven where she recharged her spiritual batteries.

As you can imagine, Ralph had a good time with the title Ali chose for herself and had calling cards printed up for her. They said "Mother Allison, Gypsy Priest, have stole, must travel."

After Ralph died Ali and I remained together and at one point we legally became domestic partners. At that point she changed her last name to mine, largely to honor Ralph, whom she considered her husband. We have a lot of fun with that, too, passing ourselves off as the notorious Williams sisters. So do Rick and June.

Ralph never let me see this manuscript until he was done. Then he gave Ali and me each a copy to read. After we had done so the three of us talked about it, mostly to clear up details. The only thing I really objected to was the title, which I thought should be The Women of My Dreams. I felt the original title left Ali out. I knew she was as dear to Ralph as I am and I felt it was unfair to her, even though the book was dedicated to the both of us. This was one of the few disagreements we never resolved, and it was Ralph and Ali who outvoted me.

Be that as it may, I do have the last word here. So I am exercising the prerogative of every woman. To set the record straight, I may have been the woman of Ralph Williams' dreams. Yet it is my beloved Ali who is, and always will be, the woman of mine. She tells me I am the woman of hers. To her way of thinking there is no higher calling. I think she's absolutely right, and I know exactly why. I think Ralph would agree, but that's another story.

www.ingramcontent.com/pod-product-compliance
Lightning Source LLC
Chambersburg PA
CBHW070445260626
47161CB00004B/1211